Bunny Suits of Death

Bunny Suits of Death:
Tales of a CSI
by
Laura A. Merz

Dedication

For Jennifer – in whom I always believed. And for my Grandmother Joyce, who always believed in me.

Disclaimer

Nothing in this book happened as it is written. Names have been altered, details of scenes have been changed, and of course, human memory is fallible. I have endeavored to keep true to the spirit of the crime scenes and experiences while shielding victims, suspects, and co-workers from any sort of literary limelight. In addition, characters became composites of people I met in real life in order to keep the cast of characters to a reasonable level.

Media Tectonics
An imprint of 4M Associates, Inc.
www.mediatectonics.com

This edition published by Media Tectonics,
Daisy Yotsuya 101, 2-9-7 Wakaba,
Shinjuku-ku, Tokyo 160-0011 Japan

ISBN: 978-4-9906172-4-0 (pbk)
ISBN: 978-4-9906172-5-7 (ebk)

Cover design by Andrew Pothecary at ForbiddenColour.com
Cover illustration by Andy Boerger
Book design by Joy Mielke

Table of Contents

Bunny Suits of Death: Tales of a C.S.I.

Acknowledgments

No memoir is ever created alone. By its very nature it is a composite of the interactions between the author and the people in his or her life. I am indebted to my Wichita Unitarians (Shala, Luca, Jamey, Jennie, Aimee, Jim, Caroline, Steve, Candy, and Susan) as well as to my wonderful co-workers on the CSI squad and on the police force; Names have been changed, but you know who you are. To James, who made me feel loved and treasured and who listened to all my stories. To my friends in college, graduate school, California and Japan who don't appear here, but who helped shape me and my sense of humor. For Jill Shapiro – the best Anthropology professor on the planet and the inspiration for my career. To my literary Agent, Cindy, who stood by this project over the years of rejections. To my family, who have always supported me, whether I'm moving across the state, the country or the world and who read countless versions of these stories as I edited them. Finally, to the men and women in law enforcement, and to crime victims everywhere – your spirit and courage and your stories resonate far and wide.

Wichita, Wichita, whatcha gotta say? I don't know where I'm
going but I'm certainly on my way. Wichita, Wichita, won't
you see me home? I'm halfway there but I'm halfway gone
— Billy Jonas, *Wichita*

❖   ❖   ❖

Radio static crackled, interrupting our political debate, which in
the true style of the times had degenerated to an "Are not!", "Are
so!" verbal tussle of wills in the crime lab office. "Rape scene at 144
Denton Court. Lab requested." I gulped. Both Pat and Patti were off,
and my name came next on the call list. Judging from the glares of
Keith and Maureen due to our now ended political tête-à-tête, their
help would likely not be forthcoming.

After six weeks of on-the-job training and coaching from Pat and
Patti, somehow I had yet to complete a scene alone. Grabbing my
windbreaker from the back of the chair, my flashlight from the
table, and the acid phosphatase field test kit I had recently put
together, I reached with full hands for the radio microphone clipped
to my shoulder … only to lose my precarious hold on all the items
and have them crash to the floor, which was broadcast to the entire
Wichita police department due to my death grip on the microphone
transmit button.

My voice came out small and squeaky, "Lab twenty-four, en
route." Pausing by the wall-sized map of the city by the lab entrance,
I looked for Denton Court. All the way south, by the Air Force base.
After tracing the best route with my finger in what would be a futile
attempt to commit the location to memory, I ran out the door.

The laughter from Keith and Maureen followed me out. It wasn't
cruel, just … amused. They knew it was time for me to be on my
own. Breathe, I told myself during the elevator ride six flights down
to the lobby, across the City Hall foyer, and into the parking garage.

The Crime Scene vans were always hot this time of year, since we weren't allowed to park them in the shade of the lower levels of the parking structure.

Breathe.

I sucked in a lungful of searing hot air and coughed until my eyes teared. Rape at 144 Denton Court.

Breathe, I told myself. Just breathe. I can do this.

CHAPTER ONE

Oompa-Loompa Land

Maggots jump.

They don't tell you this in graduate school in the lectures, and they also fail to mention it before you go into the decomp room (that's short for decomposition room, or in other words: this dead person has been dead for a long time and the body really smells awful and it's quite possible that beetles and maggots are going to come out of his eye sockets, à la whatever horror film you choose to insert here). No, what they do in graduate school is to give you a lovely diagram of the life cycle of the bluebottle fly, in which the fly larva look as if they could take center stage in the next Pixar movie and the flies themselves are winging their way to a magical land of trash cans and picnic remains. And even when they took us all to a real-life autopsy, we only saw the nicely fresh dead bodies that didn't smell, and could quite possibly have been actors auditioning for the role of Corpse #1 in Law & Order.

But the maggots in the decomp room jump. And writhe. And generally become much more menacing than the cuddly characters I met in A Bug's Life because I know that they are the reason why this body looks as bad as it does. They have been feeding on the dead man. And apparently not only is he quite tasty, but he also gave them superpowers because they're leaping up six or seven inches, which is definitely many times their body length. It's as if the Spider-man story is being told backward, and the insect bites the radioactive man and suddenly has powers beyond the ordinary larva. And this is why we're all dressed in gear reserved for only NASA people who walk on the moon, and apparently Crime Scene Investigators and Medical Examiners. I have duct tape on my wrists, binding my non-breathable, blindingly white bunny suit with a hood to my triple layer of latex gloves. We look just like the scene in the original Charlie and the Chocolate Factory, where Mike Teavee and Charlie go to the TV room to see Wonkavision in action. We are the Oompa-Loompas (minus the orange faces and green hair) in crazy white suits that are only used in clean rooms to make nuclear bombs. The song beats against my skull: "oompa loompa doopah dee doo" I think, and then wonder if other CSIs have thoughts like this when faced with dead bodies and jumping maggots. The suit even has booties attached to it, so I feel as though I'm wearing the most uncomfortable onesie ever devised. It's my third day on the job.

The people on TV tell you to breathe through your mouth in decomp rooms. The writers who say that have clearly never been in a room with a ripe dead being. Because if you breathe through your mouth, you'll taste death, and that sweet, sickly, overpowering odor tastes far worse than it smells. If you just breathe through your nose, you'll get used to it in a few minutes. If you breathe through your mouth, you'll taste it for days, and no amount of brushing will get that out. The TV shows always have people gagging and leaving the room, only to come back in a little while later, which is yet one more myth to debunk for my CSI: Miami–enthralled family and friends. Vicks under the nose also doesn't help. If you're in a room that smells awful, why would you use a product that is designed to open your nasal passages? Once you're in a decomp room, you stay in unless you have to leave for a life-threatening emergency, and vomiting doesn't count. Because once you're there for two minutes and used to the smell, you don't want to have to get used to the smell all over again.

So far, the medical examiner has spoken her notes into the tape recorder in a soft monotone and taken photographs of the body as it appears in the body bag. I haven't thrown up yet. It's helpful if you tilt your head to the side and think, "Huh," with a scientific mindset. You cannot think of this person as a person. Because if you do, you'll lose your lunch and possibly your will to do the job at hand. This person is a puzzle. A logic problem from the GRE exam:

> If Bob has been dead for three days, and his body is placed in
> a shallow grave just after he becomes deceased, how bad will
> he smell if the average temperature of the air in Wichita in July
> is ninety-four degrees?

I know I should collect the larva. They always collect the larva on

TV, and it's always really important because the larva only comes from one region of the world and isn't found naturally in the US. And then we would go on to find out that the main suspect works in the entomology department of the local university where he did his dissertation on Romanian jumping larva, and when he killed the victim, a single egg that had attached itself to the wool sweater he had been wearing (I don't know why he was wearing a wool sweater in July, but hey, that's for the writers to work out) then rubbed off onto the victim's clothing where it hatched and we collected it, and thus, it proved that the suspect killed the victim and the jury members all go, "Ooh!" when we show them the jar with the jumping larva in it because somehow the case got to trial in sixteen hours even though we didn't know the victim's identity when we started the autopsy.

But this isn't TV. And as my coworker Mike would say, "You think the city of Wichita is going to spring for a forensic entomologist to come out here and look at larva when we don't even know who the dead guy is?" And he's right. We've got a budget. That much I get already, judging by the fact that the decomp room doesn't even have a decent ventilation system. So instead of collecting larvae, the medical examiner takes a hose, sprays down the body and thousands of jumping, squirming creepy-crawlies wash down the drain. I still can't tell what race the victim is. He's so bloated and his skin is so purple that he might be albino or African American. The outer layer of his skin is already peeling off and the water from the hose helps it along. The scalpel digs into the notch between his collarbones. We found him in the park, dumped in a shallow grave. Actually, a jogger found him in the park, mainly because the grave was a little too shallow and his knee popped up out of the ground. He was in an area of the park that wasn't heavily trafficked, so it was sheer luck that someone found him as quickly as they did. At 9 a.m. the humidity was so high, it felt like we were walking through our own personal sprinkler systems. We were about to don the white bunny suits (thus, increasing the heat factor significantly) grab shovels, and start digging him out.

One thing they never show on TV is the Red Cross van that shows up at crime scenes. God bless these women and men. They know we'll be out here for a while in sunlight that would deter Burning Man enthusiasts, and so they show up, every time, with a van full of icy cold beverages, and baggies of ice for the backs of our necks. No one ever calls them, and they never intrude on the scene. They're just there, doing something that makes the job of people who deal with the horrors we inflict upon each other just a little bit better. Quiet heroes who offer smiles and orange juice. The woman in the van could tell that I was new, since she's never seen me before and I had just the faintest green tinge around my freckles.

"You'll do fine," she smiled at me. "But take this sun block and get it on before you fry yourself."

Clearly, she's a much better CSI than I'll ever be. I wasn't nearly so prepared. As we waded our way into the grave scene, passing from the browned grass of the path to the wilted greenery of the vines covering the ground, my boss called out, "You all know that's poison oak in there, right?" "We" obviously had no idea, judging from the pause in step that all four of us take, and then as one, we nodded. Because of course we knew that. Of course we wouldn't wade into a scene covered in poison oak without knowing it was there. There would be a burning of the bunny suits after this scene.

As I crouched down to photograph the knee, I could see that it was nearly skeletonized. I had no idea what that meant. The flies around the area were thick, and I didn't know decomposition rates for hot humid July weather in Wichita. Mike took soil samples that wouldn't be analyzed, while Mona started to dig gingerly around the knee to uncover the rest of the body. He had a bandanna around his thigh, which in this city means he's a gang member. As Mona dug, the smell grew.

The medical examiner finishes digging out the liver, intestines, kidneys (which are always smaller than I expect) and other internal organs. They're mostly intact, but don't hold together all that well once they're out of the body. Bacteria have started to liquefy them and the medical investigator quickly weighs them and gets tissue samples into jars before the process becomes too sloppy. So far we haven't seen anything to indicate cause of death, but we're all still betting something will come up. Mike is having problems getting fingerprints. That skin slippage I'd noticed earlier makes the fingers too slippery to roll decent prints. Plus there are still some residual maggots under the skin making it pulsate as they gorge themselves. Fingerprinting him while his skin is still on won't be possible. Mike looks at me. This person doesn't seem all that large and Mike could easily play linebacker for Michigan State.

"No, Mike. You're kidding, right?"

I know what he wants me to do. I've read about it. I've heard people discuss it, but it's my third day on the job. I'm in a decomp autopsy room with jumping maggots that No One Told Me About. I'm in a bunny suit that's made of the material from hell that doesn't breathe and sweat is rolling down my back, causing me to do the "Icky Bug Dance" every few minutes, where I feel a drop of sweat and think it's a bug that got inside my suit somehow and I flail my arms and legs about in a futile attempt to shake it from my body. (My only comfort is that the medical investigator, detective, medical examiner, and Mike have all done this shimmy a few times today as well.) And it's my third day on the job.

"Mike, I just don't know. I mean I could try it, but I'm lousy at taking prints anyway. I've never taken them from a live person, much less a dead one. No way. Just … No way."

Mike looks at the print card, at me, purses his lips, and blows out like a motorboat. He looks at his hands, at the body's hands, at the fingerprint card. Silence is a strong motivator and I capitulate.

"All right, all right. I'll give it a shot, but I'm not promising anything."

Mike steps back, still not saying anything. He hasn't spoken since we entered the decomp room. Whether he was observing me or just naturally taciturn I didn't yet know, since technically, he wasn't on my shift. But my boss thought this would be a good learning opportunity for me so he told me to come in early once the call about the grave came out over the radio. I turn to the medical examiner.

"Can you cut through the skin on the wrist? We're going to try to glove him for some prints."

Gloving, I should explain, is the lovely process whereby the skin of the hands comes off like a glove, which then enables an intrepid and soon to be traumatized investigator to put the skin over his or her own hand (fully gloved first with latex) and roll the fingerprints. The medical examiner nods, and for a split second, I catch her eye. There's no sympathy. I swear there's just a hint of amusement. We manage to pull the skin off the right hand, though the palm and back tear. It's so fragile I'm afraid to put my hand in (I'm afraid for that reason as well as the ick factor and the jumping maggots). Looking at it, this translucent membrane, only a few cells thick, and slick with what I can only think of as decomposition goo, I slowly put my index and middle fingers into the glove. Mike has the ink pad and card ready, and by holding the skin steady with my left hand, my right hand rolls a print. Unfortunately, the skin comes off with the ink and sticks to the card. It's just too fragile and it smudges. I try the middle finger with the same result. Come on! I can do this. The orange-juice lady believes in me. No luck with the ring finger either, but the pinky comes out clean and with a beautiful ulnar loop pattern. I think I can see Mike's eyes crinkle, which means he's smiling. If this person was ever fingerprinted, we'll get an ID. For a second, I want to drop the skin to the floor and make a mad desperate run for a shower. But with great deliberation, I tilt my head to the side and think, "Huh. So that's how you do that."

A loud buzz fills the room as the medical examiner fires up the bone saw to cut into the cranium. She's clearly an expert at this and makes a quick, neat incision all around the skull. Then I learn something completely new regarding human anatomy. You can fold our faces down like rubber masks and then fold them back up again when you're done working on the skull. It doesn't look at all real, which is one of the reasons Halloween masks freak me out to this day.

As she takes the top of the skull off, five enormous very fast beetles scramble out over her hand and onto the floor. Every person in the room screams and jumps. The saw has agitated them and they're desperate for cover and quiet. Mike grabs the hose and sprays them into the drain. As we stand there, sweaty, panting, hearts pounding, in the overwhelming odor of death and the sight of a decomposed body of a young man, we all burst into laughter.

"Did you see her jump?"

"My god, how fast can those things move?"

"Not as fast as you did when you saw them!"

"Hey, Mike, collect a sample of those suckers!"

I can barely stand up, and for a horrible second, I'm terrified my bladder won't hold up. The cacophony of voices makes me realize just how silent we've been for the past four hours. We've been in this decomp room all that time, and aside from the quiet dictation of the medical examiner and my protestations to Mike earlier, not a word has been spoken. The spell of death has been broken.

"We got a bullet to match the hole in the occipital!" calls out the medical investigator as he peers into the now insect-free brain case.

I snap a few pictures and take out my bullet box. It's cardboard, with cotton inside, so that no hard edges will scratch or damage the lead. The evidence stamp is already on it so as not to dent the box once the bullet is inside. After a few more photographs, the crime lab's part is done, and we're free to leave. As I step out into the fresh air with my bullet box, photographs, and fingerprint card with its perfect ulnar loop, I smile. I can do this. And it's only my third day on the job.

Fourteen hours later at the end of my real shift, I'm regaling Natalie with the story of the beetles. As we giggle, one of the detectives saunters across the hall to the crime lab.

"Identified the kid," he tells us. "From a gang up north. We rounded up the rival gang members and three of them were scratching their legs like crazy." He grins. "I guess they were never Boy Scouts. No idea what poison oak looks like."

I can hear my Homicide Investigations professor's West Virginia twang in my head, "Folks, that's what we, in investigations, call a CLUE."

Natalie, the detective, and I go from giggles to full-blown laughter. "Idiots!" I think. "Yeah," the detective finally wheezes out as he heads to the door. "Victim was thirteen."

Suddenly, the world doesn't seem so funny.

CHAPTER TWO
Forensics Always Leads to Kansas

It was the blue roof that made me realize I could move to Wichita and not die of shock. I nearly cried as the plane circled the Dallas airport and I looked out at the flat, barren, brown landscape with its dotting of nondescript brown-roofed houses that all looked as though they had been built by the same person who made my paper doll cut-out house books when I was seven.

The uniformity was overwhelming. How could I leave the East Coast for this? How could I ignore the allure of the city lights of New York? I thought Washington, D.C. was a backwater town for closing the Metro at midnight on weekdays. Moving there from New York for graduate school had been a shock to my system, ever since I hopped on the train at midnight after a late-night study session and was informed of my luck as this was the last train. "Ever?" I squeaked out in surprise. The idea of a last train just didn't compute. But move to a city with no public transportation? Never! How then was I supposed to manage in a city that not only didn't have a train system, but where the buses ran a scant once an hour? The panic started to rise and I could feel my left eye start to twitch in what I hoped was a nonthreatening manner (since appearing threatening on an airplane is never a wise choice in these modern times).

But as the plane began its descent into Wichita, I could feel the difference. Well, actually, I could see the difference. For there, below me, in all its glory, was a bright blue roof. A bright blue roof with the word "hi" painted on it in yellow letters. And suddenly the world and the Midwest didn't seem so alien after all. Someone in this town cared enough about the incoming plane people to welcome them with a message from a rooftop. Or, they were insane and welcoming the alien overlords that they were sure were going to arrive at any minute. Truthfully, either option was better than the Dallas cityscape from above.

The taxi driver smiled at me in the rearview mirror as I fiddled with my new briefcase. I felt like a fraud, like a small child playing dress-up with her parents' business accessories instead of a competent crime scene investigator about to interview for her first job after graduation.

"You want me to wait for you while you're in there?" he asked. I looked at him in astonishment. I had no idea cab drivers spoke English. Having only ever taken them in times of emergency in New York and Washington, I never expected cab drivers to speak such clear English. But one thing I did know was that I had no idea how long my interview would be, and I certainly didn't have the money for a cab to wait with the meter running. I smiled back.

"Thanks, but I don't know how long I'll be and wouldn't want to hold you up from another fare."

My cab driver laughed. "Hon, you ain't East Coast anymore. I won't get another fare for a few hours yet. Don't you worry. I'll turn off the meter."

I felt those words go through me with a warm blast. On the one hand, I couldn't imagine a cab driver in New York turning off his meter and waiting for me. It was such a nice gesture. On the other hand, I also couldn't imagine a place where a cab driver wouldn't get another call for several hours. How on earth did he make a living here?

"I'll be over here in the parking garage. My name's Ernie," he said. "Good luck in there."

I had been to Kansas once before in my life and hated it. True, I hadn't been to Wichita, but I had been to Topeka, and that was a frightening enough place. Back in high school I had been in the Forensics Club, which I was quick to point out involved the meaning of the word that lent itself to dramatics rather than dead people. I'd done a ten-minute one-woman show of A Midsummer Night's Dream that was good enough to get me to the national championship. The year before I went, it had been held in San Francisco. I wondered what exotic location would host nationals that year, only to discover with a sinking heart that it was Topeka. In truth and in retrospect, Topeka probably wasn't that bad, but the hotel we stayed in was being renovated and the water came out of the faucet a murky brown. There were spiders in the bedroom. A convention of Wizard of Oz fans happened to coincide with the forensic championships, so I saw more Dorothys and Tin Men than I really needed to. And so I stated with the firm conviction that can only be mustered up by a sixteen-year-old, that I HATED Kansas and would never, under any circumstances, live there.

I went into City Hall and received my visitor's badge from the officer at the desk before taking a deep breath, forgetting my briefcase at the desk, going back for it, and then finally walking into the interview room. A quick survey of the room told me exactly ... nothing. Beige walls, one table with fold-out legs, and four chairs, three of which were occupied by white-haired men. The one with the mustache smiled at me and from the twinkle in his eye, I knew he would be the one I spoke to when I answered questions. He looked nothing like my grandfathers, but I knew, right then, that he would be a surrogate grandpa in this strange place if I moved here.

"Did you bring a copy of your resume?" the one in the middle asked. "Yes, I did." I opened my briefcase so that they couldn't see the contents, extracted a single piece of paper, and handed it to them, along with my graduate school transcript showing full honors in Forensic Science. What they couldn't see was that once I had taken those papers out, the briefcase was empty aside from a small ceramic seal named Humphrey who was wearing a bowtie. Humphrey had been with me since I was ten years old, and had seen me through every final exam, every move, every college boyfriend and graduate school crisis. Humphrey was good luck incarnate, and with no other job prospects on the horizon due to the economic downturn after 9/11, I needed all the luck I could get, Ernie's good wishes not withstanding.

"What sort of experience do you have with footwear impressions?" I took a breath, held it, and exhaled. There were too many options— which should I choose? A shotgun approach might be the best option in a state where gun shows are regarded as family-fun outings.

"My graduate program placed a strong emphasis on crime scene techniques. For footwear, it would depend on the surface. Are you referring to casting in mud, dirt, sand, or snow? Or are you referring to two dimensional impressions in dust or dirt on a smooth surface?" I looked at the men expectantly. My "grandpa" gave what could only be described as a half-harrumph, half-chuckle, while the oldest of the three nodded. Only the middle one appeared put out by my question.

"Snow," he said shortly and made a note on the paper in front of him. "Well, I wouldn't cast anything without first photographing it and doing a detailed sketch with measurements, provided it was cold enough to maintain the impression. ..."

I watched them nod as I spoke and I hoped my intuition was right: that they would ask me to work for them. There weren't a whole lot of people clamoring to be CSIs in Wichita, Kansas, and since the TV show CSI had just come out that season, I was ahead of the wave of people who would soon be competing for the limited number of jobs out there. After all, who would want to move from the East Coast to here? They wanted the cities of New York, D.C., Baltimore, Boston, Miami. People who worked crime scenes wanted to be where there was crime, and what crime could there possibly be in Wichita? They wanted to be the people on TV who had a different murder to solve each episode. They wanted the glamour and excitement.

I just wanted a job to pay back my parents for their help with graduate school expenses and hopefully let me help people who really needed it. Lord help me, I wanted to move to Wichita because that's where the job was. My dream of working for a federal agency had been put on hold, along with my resume, due to hiring freezes in the federal government. I had clung to the hope of the Naval Criminal Investigative Service calling me to offer employment ever since I had interned there, but after six months of temp work making photocopies for corporate law firms after graduation, reality had set in. Though I loved the people there and would jump at the chance to work with them, times were tough, and few departments were looking for people. Instead, they were looking at how to trim their already stretched budgets even farther. Wichita was the answer. I just needed to adjust the question.

I called my mother to tell her the news as soon as they told me. "Mom, why does Forensics always end up in Kansas?" I asked her. The cosmic forces, having waited nine years to bring about my second trip to Kansas in the name of the other type of Forensics, laughed. But as I walked out of City Hall, Ernie's cab came to life and pulled up by the door, and the friendly officer smiled at me as I returned my visitor's badge. I thought about the blue roof. I thought about "Grandpa." Perhaps it wouldn't be so bad after all.

CHAPTER THREE

On My Own

Although I had been out to the shallow-grave death scene and worked the autopsy, it had been with many other investigators, and I was mainly supposed to observe. I hadn't actually worked a crime scene on my own. Not that I would anytime soon, as the probationary period for a new CSI lasted for nearly six weeks, and that meant I wouldn't be without a supervisor at any scene for that time frame. And I thanked all the gods in the world that I ended up on second shift with Pat as my supervisor. As surrogate grandpas go, Pat topped them all. He had stories to tell of the old days of crime scene investigation. He had helped me move into my apartment when I'd arrived with a U-Haul, my parents, and a small aquarium of two gerbils that my friend Jo had given to me before I'd left the East Coast. (The gerbils didn't last long, as one of them promptly ate the other one in a fit of rodent cannibalism that led me to work the smallest crime scene I had ever seen.) Pat taught me how to drive the huge crime scene van, when the largest thing I had ever handled before was a Toyota Tercel wagon from circa 1984 when they made them entirely out of aluminum and a stiff breeze would blow them over. I had no idea how to make a wide turn with a van, and I may have disconcerted Pat when we got into the van and I cheerfully sat behind the wheel and chirped to him "So, what do I do?" During my childhood, my mother used to perform what I call the "gasp of horror" when she would see how messy my room had become, and now it was somewhat shocking to hear it coming out of someone else's mouth. After a rather lengthy lesson on the roof of the parking garage, and then a harrowing experience on the streets of Wichita, where we were all grateful that traffic in Wichita is extremely light, I was decreed ready to go out—under supervision, of course.

But today was different. Today was the first day I would be in charge of a scene with only Pat to observe (and hopefully not interfere) as I processed it. Of course, there would be an officer at the scene for security, as CSIs aren't armed, in spite of what television says. We carried flashlights on our utility belts instead of guns. We drove enormous vans instead of squad cars with flashy lights. We are the nerds of the police department. With the exception of Pat and Jerry, who were old enough to remember and be members of the lab back when they were all also sworn police officers, the rest of us but one were people who did not seem like law enforcement material. Maureen was the only other person who seemed comfortable whether she was carrying a flashlight or a gun. Legend had it that she once vomited a little at a death scene due to the smell, but managed to keep her mouth closed and RESWALLOW it before anyone knew about it. But she also had a love of stray cats and was constantly looking for homes for them. That was how I, with my asthma-inducing cat allergies, ended up with an adorable gray ball of fluff named Pyewacket. Maureen had seen how lonely I was in Wichita, because let's face it, you don't exactly meet a whole host of nice people when you're a crime scene investigator. Most people you meet on the job are distraught and hysterical, or criminals—and quite possibly all three combined. And in spite of my patriotism, hippie liberal law enforcer doesn't go over well in a conservative police department, so I wasn't making tons of friends there either. So one day, Maureen showed up with a pet carrier and Pyewacket. That was the day I lost my heart and signed myself up for the most expensive allergy medication known to man. I couldn't say no, not when I saw that adorable gray fuzzy face and realized that I dared not refuse a woman who could swallow her own vomit.

But those concerns fled far into the back of my mind as I put the van in park next to the squad car in the parking lot. I had just arrived at the burglary site and discovered that the officer on scene was a woman my age with a friendly smile and a poise I would have given anything to have. She gave me the rundown of the scene—fairly straightforward. The balcony door on the apartment had been forced open and several electronic items, including a computer and stereo equipment, were missing. I nodded. This was it. I was ready. After striding into the apartment via the front door, I paused, looked around in a confident manner, and realized I had no idea what to do next. Where did I start? The place had obviously been ransacked, and somehow the clues didn't just jump right out at me. Back in graduate school one of my professors once put up a slide of a grocery store aisle. Every can, box, and bottle had been knocked to the floor in a colorful collage of confusion. As we all stared at the chaos on the screen, he turned to us and asked, "Okay, so where would you start looking for fingerprints?" And I remember thinking "uhhhh?" Because I hadn't a clue. If you fingerprinted every item, you'd be there for weeks, and probably get nothing more than the stock person's and discerning shoppers' prints on every item. What on earth would you do in a situation like that? I also recalled that the professor never told us what he would do in that scene. He was just showing us the slide to let us know that not every scene was as tidy as they showed on Law & Order.

As I stood and pondered, Pat came over and gently tugged at the camera strap around my neck. Of course! Photographs. Photographs would be a good start. I used up six rolls of film on that scene. Which was five and a half more rolls than were probably necessary, but it was my first scene and I wanted it to be good. The nice police officer sat down to write another page in what was becoming the most detailed burglary report in the history of the Wichita police department.

But photographs done, I next opened up my notebook and sketched the doorway. Pat assisted by measuring the door, which in truth gave me a better idea of where to focus my drawing. I've never been an artist and assumed that my death scene diagrams would involve stick figures with x's for eyes, but I really tried to draw a nice 3-D diagram of the sliding glass doors. Another hour ticked by. By the time I had the fingerprint powder out and was ready to dust for fingerprints, I had been at the scene for nearly three hours. I sprayed powder over every conceivable surface. (A minor point but one well worth noting if you ever have a CSI in your home—we don't clean up the fingerprint powder, we just spread it around. That means that after we leave, you have to go through your home and attempt to rid it of the most stubborn particles known to cleaning supplies. It might be easier if you just moved.)

I found several prints on the sliding glass door and lifted them with fingerprint tape, only to discover I had no idea how to cut the tape so that I could place the prints on the fingerprint cards we used. We had specialized cards for fingerprints known as matte acetate cards. These appeared cloudy, but when you put the tape down on the card, it would turn clear and thus you could put a number of backgrounds behind the card to help see the fingerprint better. If I used black powder on the glass because it showed up better than white powder, then I could put a white piece of paper under the card at the lab to contrast with the color of the powder. Conversely, if we were fingerprinting a dark surface, we used white or gray powder and then put a black piece of paper under the card for contrast. But none of that mattered because I couldn't cut the tape off the roll and thus couldn't properly mount the print on the card. Pat chuckled at my bewilderment and pulled out a pocketknife.

"We'll have to get you one of these," he commented. After four hours at the scene, I packed up my equipment and said farewell to the apartment owner who by now was wishing he never reported his stereo stolen. The beautiful officer, having finished her report on this burglary and all her other paperwork for the day so far, smiled and waved as she drove off.

After we got into the van, Pat gave me his critique of my work, which consisted of pointing out that 216 photographs might have been a tad excessive for that particular scene, and that he had taken the liberty of finding out the officer's name, Heather, and had gotten her number because he thought we could be friends.

As I walked back into the lab, Maureen and Patti turned toward the door. "Girl, we thought he kidnapped you, you were there so long!" I smiled, fingerprint card in hand, officer's name in my memory, and gray fingerprint powder smeared all over my uniform.

"I'll get faster," I commented before clicking on my radio to report that Labs twenty-four and three were back in the building. Turning to the computer, I settled down to type. After all, I had a five-page officer's report to compete with.

CHAPTER FOUR
Over the Rainbow

I was in love with my uniform. Not in the macho way some police officers were in love with their power or their ability to avoid speeding tickets. I loved my uniform because it meant that I belonged to something bigger than myself. I was a member of that thin blue line that helped keep law and order in a town. I was a member of a fraternity that went beyond any racial or gender lines. If someone was wearing that uniform, then they protected the innocent, went after the guilty, and fought for truth and justice. I was Superman with a fingerprint brush and a UV light source (which was sort of like X-ray vision, except it showed you things you'd really rather not see, like how often the comforters are changed on beds in budget hotels). Lab personnel even wore badges, just as sworn officers did. It shone on my nightstand. Back in college my friends and I had often disparaged "the man" and how he was oppressing us, so the 180-degree flip we had all been forced to do when I joined the blue line and became "the man" caused no end of confusion for us. I often wondered if I would now have to oppress myself. I hadn't felt these emotions when I ordered my uniforms, but when the other new investigator and I drove up north to the training grounds to get some of our gear issued to us, and they handed me my badge, I felt my eyes tear up.

In election years and in between, talk radio hosts and Republican candidates speak of liberals as those who don't love their country. They speak of us as those who would not fight for justice and who would rather throw stones at the police than help them toe the line. When they handed me my badge, and I put on my uniform, I discovered something about all the antipathy between liberals and conservatives. When I put on that uniform and clipped on that badge, it didn't matter what political leanings I had. I was serving my country to the best of my abilities, and the vitriolic words of Ann Coulter could never take that away from me.

Not that my uniform was without flaws. Dieter, the other new investigator, and I had been issued all of our gear and uniforms at the same time, and we both noticed something a little, well, odd. The long-sleeved shirts were just fine, and the short-sleeved shirts had a nice breathable material. And the pants, while suffering from flashbacks to the 1980s high-waist fashion trend, were serviceable. But the jackets … seemed a bit on the thin side. They were nothing more than windbreakers, and though the weather was anything but cold at the moment, I had heard tales of the Christmas Eve murders of the previous year that coincided with a snowstorm, and somehow, a windbreaker didn't seem like it would be much help in scenes such as those. Dieter and I brought this up to the head of the lab, who, though sympathetic, couldn't do much. Those were the items issued, and that was all there was to it. Luckily, Pat knew all the inside tricks of the department. He told us, in no uncertain terms, that we were to take ourselves to the extra storeroom of old uniforms at the training grounds up to the north of the city and see if they had anything warmer. We could get it altered to fit us if necessary. (Dieter was Dorothy to my Munchkin in size differential—but the uniforms in general fit him much more readily than me. Latex gloves in the "extra small" size are not to be used willy-nilly but instead to be treasured by the small-statured among the crime fighting forces.)

As we passed through the doorway of the storeroom, Dieter and I experienced what Technicolor must have been to Dorothy after a lifetime of monochromatic hues. Every nook, cranny, and drawer was stuffed with gems from days gone by. Want a Wichita uniform from 1957? Sure! No problem! What were they wearing back in 1933? Go check the third closet from the back on the right-hand side. We were giddily trying on coats, when my eye caught sight of the Emerald City. There, off to the side, was a winter parka that had apparently been discarded out of necessity.

"No one can wear that," said the supply keeper. "The proportions are completely out of whack." As I slipped it on, I couldn't help but notice that the shoulders fit mine perfectly, and the zipper hung just a bit above my knees. I took a step forward and promptly tripped over one of the sleeves, which had apparently been made for members of the Harlem Globetrotters.

"See," chuckled Dieter, "he wasn't lying."

"I'll take it," I retorted.

Sleeves could be taken in. I had needed sleeves taken in on every shirt I had ever bought, and the rest of it fit just fine. I waddled about, arms flapping a bit like a walrus, and grinned. It wouldn't work on any CSI show I had ever seen, but then again, I was the real thing. Bad Guys, beware, for the Hippie Liberal Law Enforcer was on the loose!

The blue lights guided me into the parking lot of the Sun Inn. 144 Denton Court was a hotel that catered to the United States Air Force members based nearby and the people visiting them. The place didn't rent rooms by the hour, but then again, since they didn't charge much for the entire night, it didn't really matter. The younger men of the air force base outside of town didn't have much to entertain them in Wichita, especially if they came from larger cities. But they always had what people called their "base groupies." Young women who wanted nothing more than to sleep with a military man. Young women who considered it their patriotic duty to sleep with them, because after all, we were in a war and they supported the troops. Sometimes problems arose because an eighteen year old airman would have sex with a fifteen year old base groupie. Even though one was legally an adult and one was not, due to the Romeo and Juliet laws and the realization that the relationship was clearly consensual, so long as the parents of the girl didn't want to press charges, all would be forgiven.

The officer at the scene looked at me and then glanced down quickly. He wiped his eyes. I had never seen an officer cry at a scene before and I felt a cold pit form in my stomach. "They just took her to the hospital for the exam," he said. "She's really ... not good." I had never known Wichita officers to be masters of understatement until that night. I took out my notebook. "Did you get any information from her before she left?" I needed to know where to focus my efforts. Just because there's a bed in a room doesn't mean the rape didn't occur on the floor, in the shower, or against the wall. I needed to know the details so I would know what I was looking for in the scene. The officer nodded. "It was on the bed. You'll see. It was on the bed and it was bad."

CHAPTER FIVE

Magic Carpets

CSIs and police officers are morbid. We're the kind of people who see a stellate pattern of a gunshot wound on the skull of a person, with brain matter falling out, and think, "Wow! I bet that was a .44-caliber at least," and then take pictures for our own personal recollection, because stellate patterns that clear are rare. We're the kind of people who, when we see a dead body that's getting to the point of advanced decomposition and has a green tinge around the abdomen, will make jokes about aliens bursting from the stomach and take bets about how long it will take for the skin to rupture and explode. So it wasn't all that surprising when Pat suggested we get ribs after a triple homicide, but that didn't make my stomach any more excited about the prospect of eating them.

"Oh … no, Pat. I really don't think so. You're kidding, right?"

Pat shook his head and blew through his mustache. He had it in his mind that he'd like some ribs for lunch, and after all, what was wrong with that?

It had started a few weeks ago. Mona on first shift had received a telephone call that there was a suspicious rug in a dumpster. "A suspicious rug?" we all thought rather incredulously. Was it lurking? Had it offered drugs to anyone? Was it professing to know state secrets it would sell for a dollar a pop? What would one even put on that report as a case category? Disreputable furniture? But the person who reported it was adamant. The rug was suspicious. It smelled like blood. This meant that Mona got to go out in the one-hundred-degree heat to do one of the CSIs' least favorite activities—dumpster diving. For though the rug might be easy to spot, who knew what else lurked in the dumpster.

As it turned out, there was nothing else suspicious, but the rug did seem to have a lot of blood on it, so it was dutifully collected and placed into evidence. We spoke of it once or twice in the ensuing week, mentioning the bloody rug in the same tone of voice one would mention gangsters who couldn't aim, and people who electrocuted themselves with sex toys. Without a crime reported, there was no chance the department would request a DNA analysis. We just didn't have the money to run lab tests for every drop of blood we came across. After all, it might have been from a sacrificial goat for all we knew. And if we requested DNA on goat blood, and the press got ahold of that information, the headlines would crucify us. We would be wasting taxpayer dollars on goat blood.

Pat infuriated Maureen by beginning to buy pies from Spears. Spears had a few locations throughout Wichita, and local police legend had it that if you bought a pie there, a murder would be committed within a week. If you consider that somewhere around thirty murders were committed each year in Wichita, it was a pretty safe bet that one would happen in about a week, since they'd occur about every twelve days anyway, statistically speaking. But Maureen was the most superstitious of the lab people, to the point where she wouldn't even look at the restaurant as she drove past, and refused to say its name. Pat buying pies there and bringing them to the lab was just his way of goading her, and giving the rest of us a tasty treat, but it certainly made everyone a little jumpy. We all knew there was a suspicious rug in the evidence locker.

A few days later the word came out that we needed to get over to a nightclub ASAP. It was mainly for documentation and photography purposes, and for some unknown reason, it had to be done right then. In the dark. And considering we had to get the electricity in the place switched off because there was standing water on the floor and sparking electrical wires all around, this did not seem like the most prudent decision. But Patti, Pat, and I made our way over there to measure the interior of the club, from wall to wall, table to table, and entrance to exit. If we needed to, we could produce a scale diagram of the club, including the placement of the tables, as we saw it that day. As I was packing up my notepad, I heard the words "triple homicide" from one of the detectives and then it was linked to the word "rug." The plot thickened.

Communication between the detectives and the lab was almost non-existent, except for the old guard, good-old-boys' club that luckily Pat belonged to. As someone who had been around forever, seen it all, and done it all, he could rehash old cases with the best of the cops, and he had at one time or other helped most of them out on investigations. Had he not told us information that he gleaned from these bull sessions, we might never know anything about the scenes we investigated. It was a frustrating situation, but not one that I had any idea how to rectify. As the newest CSI on second shift, it wasn't my place to change how we communicated. So far we had no idea how the rug and the nightclub were connected, though the detectives were now getting a broader picture of the puzzle.

They next called us out to search a massive house on the west side of town. We were looking for blood, weapons, swords, saws, Igloo coolers, and Rubbermaid containers. The house, once again, had no electricity, but it did have a couple of very hungry and uncomfortable cats, who had been using the entire place as a litter box, since they appeared to have neither food nor a place to use as a bathroom inside the residence. They also had no water. And while my love of cats and concern for their well-being was well developed, my nasal passages won out in the end. The house reeked of cat urine. I couldn't blame them for their actions, since they had been locked up for heaven knows how long, but it didn't make for a pleasant scene.

Pat and I divided up the residence and told the officers to each search a room. If they found anything of note, they shouldn't move it, but should just write down where it was, and we would collect it once certain things were finished, like sketching and measuring the entire house. Infuriatingly, even though Pat clearly knew what was going on, he wouldn't tell me or anyone else in the crime lab. It was on a need-to-know basis, and we just didn't need to know. The detectives wanted to limit the number of possible media leaks, and while I couldn't blame them for that, I did feel that a background on the case might have been useful in case I was overlooking important evidence due to a lack of understanding. Somehow the house, rug, and nightclub were connected, but I had no idea how.

The lab smelled of barbecue—maybe with the sweet kind of sauce on it. It nearly overpowered you as you walked in, but if you inhaled deeply a couple of times, the smell soon faded to the background. Mona and Mike were still there, and didn't appear as if they were leaving anytime soon. Four trays of bits of bone fragments lay on the lab table. The bones were painstakingly laid out and had been sifted extremely carefully. A forensic anthropologist from Wichita State University would soon arrive to take charge of the bones and examine them. As we waited, Mona imparted this piece of advice to me: "If you're ever going to a scene that's about a mile from where you have to park the van, make sure you bring everything you need the first time around!" I didn't ask her what had happened, but I could guess. As it was, the full story made itself known a few days later once all the arrests had been made and the detectives were free to talk about it.

There had been a triple homicide in the club, and the owner had tossed the rug due to the bloodstains. He had hacked up the bodies and put them in Igloo containers. His friends helped him out by transporting some of the coolers in their vehicles and storing them at the house I had searched, until a few days ago, when they took the body parts out to the middle of a farm owned by the suspect's family. There they held a bonfire in the middle of the field and burned the bodies. The club owner and his buddies all stupidly told their wives or girlfriends what they had been doing, and one of the girls got scared and reported the crime to the police, which was how we knew where the bonfire had been and which house to search.

The more people who know a secret, the more likely it is to come out somewhere along the line. And I guess that was what the detectives had been trying to avoid. It's not a matter of not trusting the lab personnel. It's just pure statistics, like buying pies and having homicides occur. Sooner or later, word will leak out somewhere, and the suspects might get tipped off before law enforcement is ready to respond. I still didn't like it, but at least it did make it easier to take.

What didn't make things any easier was Pat's insistence on getting barbecued ribs while the lab smelled like human barbecue. To this day, I haven't eaten a side of ribs since that afternoon in the lab where I watched Pat consume about twenty of them while the bones of humans, with the same smell, lay in the next room. CSIs may be morbid, but even I had to draw the line somewhere.

CHAPTER SIX

Unexpected Unitarians

Every so often surreal things happened in Wichita just when I needed them most. I had an eight-hour crime scene that turned out to be another mystery scene. We thought it could be a homicide, but we had no body, only a lot of blood and some of the victim's stuff. This was especially annoying coming hard on the heels of the suspicious rug. So I was a little tired and cranky and in need of something different, something unusual to lift my spirits. In New York, I'd once seen a man on a unicycle going down Broadway, along with the rest of the traffic. That seemed somewhat strange, but I thought "OK, it's New York. These things happen." But then I noticed he was holding a leash and walking a small poodle. This seemed odd. It caused me to cock my head to the side and say, "Huh!" And I'd wished one of my friends had been with me to verify the occurrence. But as I moved away from New York, I figured fewer of those sorts of things would happen. And although I did see some odd things at crime scenes, for the most part, Wichita liked to follow the norm and was so mundane it lulled you into a false sense of normality.

And then a van towing a calliope being played by someone dressed up like Uncle Sam drove by. And I cocked my head to the side and said, "Huh!" Because I did not expect to see a van towing a calliope being played by Uncle Sam drive by. It seemed somehow out of place. Maybe it was the circus, "de de deedle deedle de doo doo doo" theme that hung in the air that seemed odd, or maybe it was the fact that there wasn't a circus or elephants following this act. It was just one van, one calliope, and one man.

I don't know if they were advertising something. I never even looked beyond the calliope. But I'd like to think that they weren't advertising anything. I'd like to think that somewhere in Wichita, two people woke up and said "Hey, let's get a calliope and an Uncle Sam costume!" That thought pleased me. I'd like to know who those people were, and I would like to be their friend. I'd get a feather boa and ride on the calliope with them. We could create our own Parade-For-No-Reason. I think we would all be much happier if spontaneous parades broke out all over the city.

Luckily, I had found a group of people who would assist me in spontaneous parades and other crazy endeavors, though it took a while. I had always thought I didn't belong in Kansas, the reddest of red states, with my blue state mentality. My love of jazz clubs, piano bars, and theater was more suited to a larger city. A city that had public transportation and didn't key your car if you had a Kerry/Edwards bumper sticker on it.

Early on, I was ready to call it quits, move home, and try again. After months of loneliness in Wichita, where I felt I would never find my group, my mother gave me the best advice a woman can give her hippie liberal daughter. She told me to find religion. After all, I was living in the Midwest and that's what people did in the Midwest, right? Specifically, she told me to find the Unitarians. My mother does not take credit for helping me find the best group of friends I have ever had, because she stole this piece of advice from her mother, when she went off to college at Penn State. Central Pennsylvania and Wichita have a lot in common in that they're both relatively isolated populations and far from the sights and sounds of the New York suburbs where my mother grew up. So she found the Unitarians at Penn State and embraced the liberal religion that basically thought it might be a good idea to stop worrying about the afterlife and start making the here-and-now life better for everyone.

And now she advised me to do the same thing. I felt extremely uncomfortable just walking up to a church, since I had been happily removed from religion for a number of years, but as I approached their bazaar, which happened to be on the day I visited the church, I noticed a bumper sticker table with slogans such as "Well behaved women rarely make history!" and "Somewhere in Texas, a village is missing its idiot." After five months of a stifling police-officer, conservative-Republican atmosphere, this felt like a waft of fresh air.

A tall loud woman named Susan bore down on me with the determination of a bird of prey. She smiled. "You're new. Come and get some food."

This boded well. College and graduate students never turn down free food, and I wasn't far enough removed from that setting yet to hesitate. Jim, Aimee, Shala, Steve, and another Susan introduced themselves to me and invited me in for the service. No one told me that newcomers were supposed to get up and introduce themselves during church, but luckily Unitarians are extremely forgiving about social gaffes such as getting up and saying "Hi, I'm Laura. Umm... I don't know what to say." And then sitting back down. They chuckled politely and the minister, whose name was Carolyn, spoke about food shortages and the need for volunteerism. Amen! I thought. There's a sermon I can support.

After the service and a group hug, which was wonderful for many different reasons, not the least of which being I hadn't had a hug in months, I had to leave for work, where I had an aggravated assault/murder/suicide to deal with. Three different scenes, one very bad man. As far as anyone could tell, he went off the deep end and decided to kill his ex-wife and any men she had ever slept with. He stabbed her and killed her current boyfriend, and then he got into a standoff with the police that ended with him shooting himself in the forehead. He had this really classic stellate pattern on his head where the bullet entered. It was textbook. He had the four-point star where the gases from the gun exploded back out the entrance path of the bullet, burns around the edges of the wound, and tons of very red oxygenated blood. His brain was falling out of the wound in pieces, which was also really interesting to observe. And we were all standing around admiring the wound before any of us even thought, "Hey, we're really macabre." But we know that. Because this is what we do all day long and the only way to deal with it is to have a really dark sense of humor and to go "Huh!" in a dispassionate, scientific kind of way and find a group of people who will hug you when you really need it. I hoped the hugs and the calliope would be regular occurrences.

CHAPTER SEVEN

Dropping Acid

The small circular tin in my palm seemed so innocent, as did the words from my supervisor when he spoke them several weeks earlier.

"That's for your acid phosphatase test kit."

I smiled automatically. "Hey, thanks, Pa ... t."

Somewhere in the middle of his name, my brain kicked in. Acid phosphatase is a chemical in semen. We had chemicals to do field tests for semen at rape scenes, but the life span of one of the solutions is notoriously short and sensitive to temperature, so we kept our chemicals separate and mixed them at the scene to ensure the mixture was as fresh as possible. And since defense attorneys are notorious for checking up on lab procedures, we always tested a new mixture at the scene to ensure it reacted to semen. Pat had just handed me a tin of about fifteen tiny squares of filter paper for my test kit. Known semen samples for field testing.

Which raised the question, did my boss really just hand me a tin of his sperm? His dried sperm on filter paper? Miss Manners doesn't tell you how to handle these sorts of situations. Emily Post never once mentions it in any of her books. And though I was grateful for the gift, because really, I didn't know anyone in Wichita and where else would I have gotten my own samples, how exactly should I thank my boss? It isn't as if Hallmark has its own set of greeting cards for this sort of thing. The other investigators were all luckier. They were either male or married women, or at least ones with boyfriends, and could all obtain known semen samples without difficulty. I tucked the tin in my evidence locker, and promptly went back to my desk to the amused eyes of Patti, my southern belle co-worker.

"Lord, did Pat just give you an acid phosphatase sample?" she asked as she rolled her eyes. I nodded, caught her eye, and we both started to giggle.

"Well, honey, I don't suppose you know anyone else here yet to ask, but by the time that runs out, you'd better have a boy waiting in the wings. You don't want to go asking for a second sample."

She was filing her nails with an emery board as she spoke, but the twitch of her mouth showed the barely suppressed laughter at the absurdity of the conversation. The horror of actually asking Pat for another … contribution hadn't even crossed my mind, but surely, hopefully, I wouldn't have that many sexual assault scenes before I found a boy to assist me in these types of endeavors. There were a number of little filter paper squares in that tin. It would be fine.

The Vagabond was my favorite place to unwind after a day slogging through crime scenes. Half coffee-shop, half bar, with a waitstaff and clientele made up entirely of the seventeen people who represented the hippie liberal counterculture population of Wichita, it felt completely like home there. Back in high school and college, I was a theater girl. A drama queen/gothling (what the true Goths called the girls and boys who just went around wearing black and decrying the world as a bleak and miserable place). Being a member of a police department, being part of "the man" who clearly violated every principle of freedom and personal choice I held dear, had never been an option I remotely considered for my future. No, I was going to be an artist, though I could not draw; a poet, though I couldn't figure out metaphor or rhyme to save my life; or an actress, though I was truly a terrible waitress. Once I realized that these limitations might somehow hamper my creative career aspirations, I contented myself with hanging out where the creative people, the disenfranchised folk, chose to congregate. And in Wichita, that meant the Vagabond. It felt like a little piece of New York—an oasis in the desert of Wichita.

The tables were small, dark, and wooden. Candles lit the interior, and board games, Internet connections, and couches filled the back room. Lingering was encouraged. Artwork from local artisans covered the walls, and posters for the latest unknown rock band coming through town blanketed the bulletin boards. The bartenders were my age and all extremely cute. And because Wichita was still a small town, despite the population's size, everyone there knew me as the CSI girl by the second time I dropped in. I felt like Norm from Cheers. I'd open the door and the most adorable bartender, Pete, would smile from behind the bar.

"Chai tea?" he'd ask. I grinned. From day one they knew that I'd be eschewing the Long Island iced tea in favor of the infinitely better tasting and non-alcoholic chai variety. Even if I didn't know anyone else in the place, I could always sit at the bar and tell them my stories from the day. And let's face it, a CSI nearly always has interesting stories. It probably also helped that I tipped more generously than most. (Being a horrible waitress had made me that much more sensitive to the need for tips in the service industry.)

I loved the Vagabond. If I had a late night staring me in the face, I could call them up and tell them I'd be by in three minutes and Pete or Brent would be standing outside, no matter the weather, with a hot chai in his hands. The huge blue crime scene van would trundle past, and I'd reach out the window, grab the cup, and head off with a wave and a thankful smile. I didn't have to pay. They knew I'd be by later to settle the bill and let them in on whatever had happened to cause my excursions in the wee hours of the morning. Because if you went to the Vagabond, you weren't a customer. You were family.

The spate of rape scenes began the week after my boss generously handed me the tin of his seed. Patti was next on the call list for the first one, but I went along in another van to observe and assist as needed. The next one came about forty-five minutes later, and so off I went, with Pat following, since I wasn't yet working scenes on my own. Numbers 3-6 happened later that day as Patti, Pat, and I raced to keep up. By the time the seventh scene was called in, we began telling them to hold for third shift, since they'd be on in a few minutes. The next few days were the same way.

"What's going on?" I asked Pat.

He shrugged. "They come in spurts," he explained. "You'll have weeks where nothing happens at all, and weeks where all hell breaks loose. You just have to roll with it."

He hitched up his pants, which did no good at all, since they were forced low due to his enormous protruding stomach, and blew through his white walrus mustache. "You'll get used to it."

I hated that phrase. I didn't think I wanted to get used to rape scenes. Shouldn't each one mean something to me? Meanwhile, my supply of filter paper was dwindling rapidly.

I was in a dour mood that night at the Vagabond though I was trying not to show it, since Pete was tending bar and I had a huge crush on him. But four rape scenes that day had sapped most of my will to smile and I toyed with the straw in my empty chai.

"Hey, Laura, what's wrong?" Pete's friendly grin usually made my heart melt, but that night, I had bigger problems on my mind.

That evening I had used my next to last piece of filter paper. One lone little scrap remained in the tin. How the hell was I going to ask my boss for new supplies?

"Oh, just stupid work stuff." I tried to brush it off, but Pete perked up. Stupid work stuff from the only CSI to patronize the Vagabond generally meant a story. Most of the other clients spent their time either in college classes or in generous people's garages, as they tried to perfect that one song that would rocket their band to stardom, and their woes just weren't as interesting.

"Come on, tell me." He cocked his head to the side in his best imitation of a bartender ready to lend an ear.

"I'm out of known samples for my acid phosphatase kit," I grumbled under my breath. I never had been a very good liar, so stating the exact truth in a way where the science obscures the embarrassing meaning seemed the best option. But Pete would not be deterred.

"Acid phosphatase? Cool. What's it for?" And so I explained. About my boss and his samples. About rape scenes and the chemicals needed to field test. About testing the chemicals needed for the field test. And about my complete lack of ability to produce the necessary sample on my own. Pete's head, still tilted to the side, but with the expression of a confused dog, nodded along with my tale.

"So ... you test the known ... sample, and what happens?" he asked.

"It turns pink." I responded. "The darker the pink, the more phosphatase in the sample." By this point, Brent and Dominick, a bespectacled, thin, adorable bartender and a patron, respectively, were also listening in.

"I bet mine would be pinkest," Brent said with confidence. Pete looked at him in disbelief.

"You think you'd be pinker than me? Dude, mine would be fucking magenta!"

Dominick laughed. "You're both punks. I'd win hands down."

"Hands got nothing to do with this little test," Pete countered.

I stared at the three boys and thought how amazing it was that young men could turn anything—and I mean anything—into a competition.

"You wanna put your boys on the line, big guy?" Dominick

challenged. Normal people don't have these conversations, I thought. Normal people go to a bar and smile at the cute bartender and hope he'll buy them a drink. Normal people don't go out to their car, drive down the block to the crime lab, and come back with three pieces of filter paper, chemicals, and paper bags so their favorite bartenders and patron can go jerk off in the bathroom of the Vagabond to find out whose semen has the most acid phosphatase in it.

Oh, dear god, please let them wash their hands before they start serving drinks again, I prayed.

Pete went first, and came out about five minutes later with an extremely satisfied look on his face. Brent went next, followed by Dominick. Each boy came out with a flat paper bag with a rather sticky piece of filter paper inside of it.

"Okay, I, um, I just want to say that phosphatase has no bearing on sperm count, virility, or any other sexual prowess or skill set," I hedged. "It's just a chemical found in semen. It doesn't really mean anything."

The boys all nodded. They looked at me expectantly. I cut off a little corner of Pete's paper and placed a drop of solution on it. A nice shade of rosy pink emerged, which prompted a fist pump and a "Check that out, baby!" from contestant number one.

Brent was next and to our mutual surprise, his turned that shade of magenta Pete had boasted about. "Aww, yeah, my boys got some spunk!"

Dominick's sample matched the color of Pete's, thus making Brent the clear winner. His bragging rights assured, Brent quickly made his way to the tables to show off his prize-winning sample. Pete leaned over the counter and looked me in the eye.

"So … problem solved, yeah?" I smiled. "Yeah, between the three of you, I've got enough known product here to last for quite a while."

A booth in the back corner erupted with a cheer of "Acid phos-face! Acid phos-face!" with Brent leading the pack. Pete placed a fresh chai tea in front of me and I leaned down low over it, shoulders shaking, as laughter took hold. I knew I would never ask him out on a date, but that was all right by me. After all, at the Vagabond, we were family.

CHAPTER EIGHT
Can I Get That To Go?

The ATM lay in a pile of rubble at my feet. "Huh," I said. I tilted my head to the side in a scientific way as I said it. This did not help. Because the ATM remained in the pile of rubble, which was several feet away from where the remains of the bank wall were now located, and I did not have a brilliant idea come to me about how I was going to move this behemoth of a machine back to the lab to fingerprint it.

True, I had been working out recently, but the weights I used in my training were of the five- and ten-pound variety, and I would need to increase that exponentially if I was going to be able to lift this thing into the van, drive it to the lab, get it out of the van, to the elevator, and up to the sixth floor. I had a dolly at the lab I could use to wheel it about, perhaps, but how was it going to get into my van in the first place? Archimedes once said that if you gave him a lever long enough and a place to stand, he could move the world. I looked about for a lever, knowing it was a dumb idea. But there's never a Swedish bodybuilder named Sven around when you need one, and right then my options were limited.

It was time to take action. It was time to blame the criminals for their misdeeds. Because this was the criminal's fault. Had he merely left the ATM in the wall of the bank, instead of hauling it out of the wall with a chain attached to a large piece of construction equipment, I wouldn't be in this predicament. I sent a silent curse out to all the inconsiderate criminals who didn't think about the poor CSIs and police who had to deal with the aftermath of their nefarious deeds.

Terry Pratchett had the right idea about criminals. They needed to be unionized. His thief's guild was a brilliant idea. People pay their yearly dues to the guild and in turn, they are not burglarized or robbed that year. If a non–guild member does rob them, you can bet the thief's guild will hunt them down and make sure that person understands that he or she cannot cross the guild and get away with it. It's organized crime at its best and funniest.

"You got a plan?" the officer asked me.

"I need either a mafia don or a giant stick," I told him sourly. He backpedaled furiously. "Okay, you take your time. You're the expert."

Peter Finchly had gotten out of jail a few weeks earlier. The detectives had all been hyped up and I couldn't figure out why until someone explained that Peter happened to be a master criminal. A master criminal of the type that Pierce Brosnan or Sean Connery might battle in a Bond movie, though without the lasers and the cars that turn into helicopters. What they meant was that Peter Finchly had style. He burgled with flair and never did the same sort of job twice. He was always experimenting. Always trying out a new way to get into houses or disarm security systems. Peter Finchly had the respect of the detectives because he never left any evidence of his presence and he always pushed the creative limits. The only reason they had caught him was a simple piece of bad luck at the last house he had broken into. As he fled with the valuables, he twisted his ankle when he stepped off the curb wrong. Even that wouldn't have been his downfall, but for a patrolman who just happened to turn onto the street at that moment. The call of a burglary had just come out over the radio, and Peter Finchly was nabbed with over $5,000 in money and jewelry on his person.

They could never prove he had done any of the other burglaries, even though they knew that he had been the one behind them, partly because he just seemed the kind of person who was that good at covering his tracks, but mostly because as soon as he was arrested, the creative, completely impossible-to-solve streak of burglaries in the more affluent areas of Wichita stopped. But he pled to a single count and was given two years behind bars. Eighteen months later, because he had been a good boy in prison, they were letting him out. Word had gone out to all the patrol officers that they needed to watch certain neighborhoods more carefully. There was talk of putting more people on the streets and possibly cancelling vacations for the time being, but those ideas were eventually seen as detrimental to the morale of the department and were shelved. Peter's picture was passed out to everyone, and the newcomers were briefed on tricks he had used in the past. Peter Finchly had every officer in Wichita on edge forty-eight hours before he would even be out of jail.

"You think you and another officer could lift it?" I asked the officer next to me. He looked at me.

"Maybe," he replied, "if the other officer was a bodybuilder."

"Yeah," I nodded, "but Swedish guys are in short supply here."

He looked at me oddly. "No, I mean if we got one of the bodybuilders on the force out here then we should be able to do it."

"We have bodybuilders on the police department?" I asked. I suppose I shouldn't have been surprised. After all, officers have to be in good physical shape, and it is a macho, testosterone-laden job, especially in the Midwest with its somewhat antiquated views of gender roles. But most of the time when I saw police officers, they were in their full gear, which included bulletproof vests. And while those vests save their lives and keep them protected, they're bulky and don't have the slimming effect of, say, vertical stripes or a well-tailored suit. And although my one cop buddy Dave was certainly handsome and fit, he wasn't a bodybuilder. But there had to be a few on the force, so I called into dispatch to see if they could scare me up a few.

"Hey, Megan, I need an available officer who's a bodybuilder," I called out over the radio.

"Honey, who doesn't?" she shot back.

I couldn't help but laugh. "No seriously, I really do need one, to help lift some evidence into the van."

"Ah." Megan knew every police officer on the force, no mean feat considering there were several hundred of them, and she also had the ability to check her computer to see who was on shift, who was on a call, and who was available to come help me. "Gotcha. Sending two units your way."

I thanked her, and the officer and I sat down to wait. I suppose I really didn't need to take the ATM into evidence. After all, I could fingerprint it at the scene ... but I didn't want to leave it in the middle of the sidewalk with all the rubble, and since this was technically a bank building, the FBI would probably want it. It was best to be on the safe side, especially when the safe side involved making fun of bodybuilding officers that I was going to refer to as Sven One and Two in my head.

In the weeks since he had been released from prison, Peter Finchly had reported in to his parole officer every day. He was always on time, always neatly dressed, always humbly sorry for the trouble that he seemed to have caused everyone with his one scrape with the law, because he never admitted to more than the one burglary. In the week since Peter Finchly had been out of prison, there had been four burglaries in upscale neighborhoods around town, each one with a different modus operandi, and each one completely devoid of any signs of who might have done such a dastardly deed. It was indeed a puzzle, answered Peter, when he was brought in and interrogated by the burglary detectives. Who knew why some people couldn't live a fine upstanding life, such as he was now doing? He had a job, supposedly, but working as a bicycle courier allowed him lots of free time to roam and provided him with an excuse to be in the more exclusive parts of town. The detectives had to let him go. They had no evidence he had done a single thing wrong. It was my job to find some.

Some women find men who lift heavy things to be sexy. I am not one of them. All I cared about was getting the damn ATM into my van, so I could take it back to the lab, so it could be processed for fingerprints. Watching the muscles bulge and hearing the officers grunt as they first hefted it upright and then slammed it down in the back of the crime scene van wasn't my idea of paradise. Not that I would ever say such a thing to Sven One, though I might to Sven Two as he had a bit too much of an ego for my taste. But at last it was loaded in and I was off to the lab, at which point the thought crossed my mind, how will I get it out of the van? Luckily, there was always an officer on duty at the desk in City Hall, and with any luck another one or two might be around as they dropped off evidence, switched shifts, or escorted prisoners. It would be fine. Just breathe. There was always help around if I needed it.

Back at City Hall, after two kindly officers pushed the ATM from the van onto a dolly, I attempted to wheel it inside. I don't know if you've ever wheeled something as heavy as an entire quarter wall of a building, but my body was probably past a forty-five degree angle as I put everything I had, including all my body weight, behind that handle, only to have the dolly move an earth-shattering three inches before hitting a crack in the cement and deciding this would be a good place to stop. I really didn't want to call the officers back. After all, I had just thanked them and sent them on their way. It would be too embarrassing to have to call them back after I waved and said, "Don't worry, I've got it from here." I had to save face. And if saving face meant breaking my spinal column, then so be it.

Thirty minutes later, I staggered off the elevator triumphantly, and possibly maimed for life, behind an ATM. Patti and I wheeled it over to the corner where it hulked menacingly as we looked for any surface that might have kept any fingerprints. Pulling the ATM out of the wall with a machine was one thing, but to get inside it, and to work some of the electronics to get to the money, I was pretty certain that you'd have to remove any gloves you might have worn. If there were fingerprints, they would be on the inside of this giant cash box. And that was where we found them. Two prints, slightly smudged, but enough for a comparison with a known suspect. And enough for our fingerprint comparison expert Mandy to come back with the news that Peter Finchly might have some explaining to do once the officers hauled him back in.

When she told the burglary detective the news, he came over and promised roses and chocolates for everyone in the lab. He wanted to thank us for all our hard work and he might even spring for a pizza! Normally, such generosity would be welcomed with open arms and a possibility that I would also ask for balloons in celebration. But right then I had more pressing things on my mind. "Hey," I called out to him, "do you think the FBI will come pick this thing up tonight?"

The officer and I measured the room together to move the scene along. As we went, we told jokes to each other. Three guys walk into a bar. The fourth one ducks. He didn't get it until I mimed banging my head into a bar.

A blonde goes into a New York City bank and asks if she can put up her Rolls Royce as collateral for a $50 loan for six months. The bank manager grins and thinks to himself "dumb blonde!" as he signs the papers. Six months later she comes back, pays him his $50 and an extra $2.50 in interest. The banker hands her back her keys and then can no longer contain himself.

"Madam, if you had a Rolls Royce, why would you need a $50 loan? You clearly have money." She smiles at him.

"Where else could I park my car for six months and be assured of its security in this city for only $2.50?"

This is why we don't use audio recordings on crime scenes. Because we see things that normal people don't see and to deal with it, we make jokes. We talk about other things. We mock the dead person at our feet. Lennie Briscoe, upon discovering a dead person in a mall, quips, "She shopped till she dropped," and we laugh because it's on TV.

But when that's your child lying in the road, you don't want the investigators to laugh and joke at the scene. You want us to be serious and focused. We are focused, but we need the black humor to keep us going. We have to laugh or we'll cry, and once we start to cry, we'll burn out and leave the job for something where we don't witness human misery every day. We'll stop fighting the good fight, because we'll lose the will to continue the scene and solve the case. So we joke. And we never, ever, have audio recordings at our scenes. Because we mean no disrespect to the dead or hurt or bereaved. We joke to each other so we will be able to come in tomorrow and do the same exact thing all over again.

CHAPTER NINE

To Boldly Go

Dave winked and motioned me over to the side of the house. "This one should be right up your alley, girl! They're Trekkies."

Trekkies? I thought. But Trekkies don't stab each other. They sit around in uniforms and pretend to be Kirk or Riker or one of the other characters who always gets the scantily clad female at the end of the show. I don't like it when people with nerdy habits commit crimes, because I tend to have nerdy habits and those sorts of things nearly always reflect badly on the nerd community. We as a society have a fascination with the bizarre, so the news and tabloids tell us about the freaks who only speak Klingon to their kids, but never mention the rest of the viewing public who watch the show, maybe buy one of the books, and then go about our daily lives without any problem functioning in normal settings. Besides, I had been completely in love with Wesley Crusher when I was twelve. Here was a boy, not much older than me, who could, if he so needed, do reverse polarity conversion equations in his head in order to save the Enterprise, and I thought that was the sexiest thing imaginable. "Wow, he's good at math," my twelve-year-old self thought, "that's so dreamy ..."

It's true. You can tell who the nerds are at a young age. But Dave's mirth not withstanding, I had a job to do. Patti and I went into the house and looked around for the signs of Trekdom, only to find none, at least in the living room. A pitiful "Meow!" from under the table caught our attention, and Patti bent down to get a better look at the speaker.

"Aww, come here kitty, kitty. ... Oh Lord! What is that?!" The alarm in her voice startled the officers on scene and I peeked over the couch to see what I thought was a cat, but the fur was so matted and tattered it was difficult to tell. One eye and an ear were definitely missing, and it almost looked like a tumor had created a second tail, though that turned out to be just one giant fur ball. It also appeared to have a drool mechanism that rivaled the Niagara Falls.

"O … kay. Hey, Patti, what do you say we take a look at the scene?" Patti and I backed away from the feline and looked around. Dave had already briefed us. It was a family affair—mother, new husband, and mother's son from the first marriage. The son was a large boy of seventeen years, so I was told, and during his mom's birthday celebration, his stepfather picked a fight with him, saying he couldn't have any of the birthday cake due to his new diet. Stepfather and stepson came to blows until they arrived at the study, where the stepfather stabbed his stepson. Ambulance called, both men expected to be discharged that night, one with a broken nose, one with stitches in his side. I couldn't help but feel bad for the unspoken victim, the mother, in the case.

The candles on the cake were still burning when we arrived. We took a look first in some of the common areas. There were overturned chairs and a few knick-knacks that had been knocked off their stands onto the floor. The house was generally tidy. No signs of Trekkieness here, though the penchant for unicorn collectibles was quite noticeable. I decided that was probably the influence of the female of the house. We observed the various knives scattered about, including the one with just a bit of frosting on it from the cake, but didn't see signs of blood. I looked at Dave and he jerked his head toward the study.

"Oh … lord." Somehow I managed to pick up Patti's curse word usage, which consisted only of varying tones of the words "Oh, lord." If used properly they could convey anger, dismay, rage, acquiescence, surprise, and happiness. When said with her soft southern accent, it sounded charming, old-world, and graceful. I just sounded tired.

The study was Star Trek central. Every wall had floor-to-ceiling display cases, every flat surface had a Plexiglas box, and when I accidentally bumped the computer mouse, it made that chirping sound Kirk's communicator made when he opened it. And over it all was blood spatter. All over the cases, the computer screen, and the desktop. It had dripped on the floor, and one arc of spatter had made it to the ceiling, most likely from the stabber's arm movement as he pulled the knife out in a sweeping motion.

Photographing bloodstains on clear surfaces is a special kind of pain for CSIs. The camera really, really wants to focus on the item inside the case, or on the other side of the glass, rather than on the dots of blood on the surface. Before the switch to digital cameras, it was not uncommon to get a roll of film back from the developer of twenty-four pictures of pretty items inside a window, that were marred by a brownish blur on the glass. Of course, that brownish blur was what we had been trying to document.

After switching over to manual mode for focusing purposes, I started taking pictures as Patti measured and sketched. This wasn't really the crime of the century, since the suspect had confessed, the witness confirmed the story, and the victim's injuries just needed a few stitches. And though I knew how to use string and lasers to find the place in the room where the stabbing occurred, it just wasn't needed this time around. From all accounts the victim, at seventeen, was much larger than his stepfather and had broken his stepfather's nose, prior to the stabbing. Self-defense might even have been an option, if it ever went to court. We were all betting that no one would press for prosecution. But where was the weapon? There was no knife lying around. There was no smoking gun. Just a room filled with miniature Enterprises, figurines in blue, red, and gold uniforms, tricorders, communicators, and other gadgets of the 23rd century.

"Hey, Laura?" Patti called. I turned and looked where she was pointing. "Oh … Lord." They had put it back in the case. There, next to the door, was a Klingon weapon called a bat'leth. It had handholds along the curved handle, and four very large, sharp spikes on it. The blood on that case was on the inside and was dripping off one of the spikes. They had put it back in the case, on the stand. What had they been thinking? That it looked more realistic with blood on it? That we wouldn't take it just because it was in a display case? That the Plexiglass would shield it from our view?

Don't get me wrong, it was a nice bat'leth, as far as I knew. I had only seen them on the TV show, but this one looked the same as those and just as lethal. I took some photographs as Patti pumped me for information, such as, how did I know it was called a bat'leth, and how much of a nerd was I really? Had I ever been to a convention? Dressed up like a character for Halloween? Did I know how to spell bat'leth? This last one gave me pause, and I frowned as my forehead scrunched up. How did one spell bat'leth? I knew there was an apostrophe, but where did it go? I had a vague idea that there might be two letter a's next to each other, and that maybe it went between them. This was actually important for the evidence custody document. It doesn't look so good when you go up in court and testify that you listed a piece of evidence as a "curved pointy thingy with spikes." Juries and defense attorneys like their CSIs to be professional and the words whatchamacallit, thingy, thingamabob, and doohickey are not permitted.

There was only one option available to me. I whipped out my cell phone and hit number three on the speed dial. "Hey, William, really quickly, how do you spell bat'leth?" I asked when he picked up the phone.

"Bat apostrophe leth," said the confused and sleepy voice of my college friend William, another fully functional Trekkie who spends his days at investment firms explaining why stock market prediction is really impossible, otherwise all the economists at colleges would be multi-millionaires.

"Thanks, I'll call you later," I answered and hung up. Patti stared at me in concern.

"You have a friend on speed dial for all your emergency Star Trek questions?" I shrugged.

"Yeah, well, you never know when you might have the need." My sister probably would have known too, but I figured I'd spare her the ignominy if she ever came out to Wichita to visit.

From the crime scene van, we carefully took out a flattened cardboard box, which was the only thing large enough to encompass the now accurately spelled bat'leth. As we looked around one last time for anything else we might have missed, I thought back to the birthday girl, a woman whose son had punched her husband, and whose husband had stabbed her son. She hadn't had a chance to eat her cake or even blow out the candles. She was instead caught between two men she loved who clearly hated each other and who decided their petty arguments were more important than her celebration. Something just wasn't right here.

"Hey, guys!" I called to the officers outside guarding the scene. "We're done in here. Let's get this furniture back up." We righted the chairs and put the unicorns back on their tables. I knew we couldn't really wash the blood off the study walls, but I had a hunch she didn't use that room too much anyway. As we left, the glow of the birthday candles caught my attention. I closed my eyes, said a silent apology for stealing a birthday wish, and blew. As we left the house, Patti paused.

"What'd you wish for? Your very own Klingon arsenal?" she asked with a smile.

"Just... that she have a better birthday next year."

Patti removed her latex glove and patted my shoulder. "Oh, lord, girl. Oh, lord."

CHAPTER TEN
Life Support

Dave stared at my neck, his eyes wide with horrified curiosity. I felt like a car accident on the other side of the highway divider. He reached out a hand and very hesitantly ran his fingers down below my tilted jaw line. I imagined I could feel the ridges of his fingerprints. He had mainly ulnar loops—quite a common sort of print. I knew because I had classified his prints for him once when we first met.

Ulnar loops are fingerprints where the ridges loop up in the middle but open up on the side of the arm where the ulnar bone is. Loops that open up toward the radius bone in the arm are called radial loops. Forensic scientists are good at many different things, but creativity in naming is not one of their strong points. I concentrated on his ulnar loop patterns to stop from wondering what it was he was feeling under them. I kept my head tilted in a slightly scientific way, but couldn't squeeze the words out past the built-up tears in my throat that I had been swallowing for too long. Dave, luckily, supplied them for me.

"Huh," he breathed. "So that's what cancer feels like."

The day before, I had been in Dr. Goodnight's office. I'd had trouble with my thyroid since graduate school, when they put me on a medication that would help the ailing organ produce more of the enzyme that among other things controls your metabolism. I had lived in hope that this medication would magically help me lose the five pounds I wanted gone from my frame by speeding things up, but that miracle cure had never materialized. After the latest round of blood tests and a biopsy for some pesky benign growths, I was ready for my medication to be updated. Dr. Goodnight, however, had other considerations.

"You need to see a specialist, Laura. You need surgery. Look, the latest round of tests came back inconclusive but suggestive of cancer—that largest growth has a diameter equal to a quarter and it's on its way to half-dollar size."

I knew this. I knew it, because I could see the lumps in my neck in the mirror when I tilted my head in a scientific manner, which I did fairly regularly.

"Here, let me pull up your latest ultrasounds and show you." She turned to her computer. I sat there dumbly wondering what people said to her at the end of the day: "Goodnight, Dr. Goodnight"? Would people try to avoid the expression by wishing her a nice evening? I tried to focus.

She continued, "You've got growths now all over your thyroid, it really is best to have it removed before something spreads to your lymph nodes."

I nodded. Breathe, I told myself. Just breathe. You will get through this. Don't cry. You are 24 years old; 24 year olds don't cry. You are an adult. I wanted to ask pertinent questions about the biopsy. I had Googled the various word combinations since learning about the growths a few weeks ago. "Thyroid tumors," "thyroid cancer," "thyroid lesions." I had checked WebMD, looked up journals on Medline. I was prepared. I was a grown-up. Dr. Goodnight looked at me for a second over the ultrasound-filled computer screen, and her face softened. Her eyes concerned, she put down my folder.

"Laura, can I get you something?" she asked. "Is there someone who can drive you home?" I wanted to tell her I was fine, that I wanted to discuss dates for the surgery. That I would handle the arrangements. That I was a grown-up. The tears came without warning, spilling over my eyelids.

"I want my mom," I sobbed into my hands.

But my mom lived fifteen-hundred miles away and I didn't want to call her until I could at least speak well enough through the sobs to make myself understood. Instead, I went shopping to see if retail therapy would work for me. The girl at the shop was bubbly. Dr. Goodnight had mentioned I might want some pretty scarves to cover up the scar on my neck until it healed, so there I was, at a hat and scarf shop, conveniently located across the street from the Vagabond. I had seen the clerk at the Vagabond before, but we had never spoken.

"I need some scarves. ..." my voice trailed off. She nodded.

"Sure, what color?"

"Something to go with everything." I said gloomily. "I'm going to have a big scar. … I might have cancer and need something to cover up my neck."

It all came out in a jumble. I don't know what I was expecting, whether it be sympathy, an empathy discount, or a gasp of horror.

"Sure. Why not something in blue? And I'll show you how to tie it over your head in a cool cover-up for when you go bald," she chirped at me.

I blinked. This I was not expecting. But I felt the knot in my stomach loosen just a fraction. I've never been good at receiving sympathy. I can argue with someone all day, or take insults and toss them back, but have someone say, "Oh, poor Laura," and I won't be able to stop the tears no matter how much I might want to. I hadn't stopped crying really since getting the news, although by the time Dave's hand came in contact with my skin the outer tears had dried and only the internal ones flowed unabated. So the practical, very matter-of-fact advice about headscarf-tying for when radiation would make my hair fall out felt like a relief. Cloying expressions of sorrow could wait for another day. Today, I had scarf-tying to learn, and then I would go to church and talk with my Unitarians.

Unitarian services have a joys and sorrows section that always confounds the congregation and minister alike. Anyone can go up and share something happening in their life, and we like to hear about the important events, but go on too long and risk the ire of people who have other places to be and a minister who must now shorten a sermon. I had not yet gone up despite months of faithful attendance. Today I joined the line.

"Hi… I'm Laura. I have a sorrow—I found out this past week that I might have thyroid cancer." A gasp from the congregation, or was that my imagination? "They're operating on Thursday."

That was all I could get out without tearing up. Luckily Carolyn, our minister, put an arm around me, and I leaned into her for a minute. Her arm was soft and pulled me into her folds, not a rock of comfort, but a security blanket wrapping me up. Somewhere in the back of my mind I was dimly aware that she wasn't fond of the advice and sympathy part of ministerial work, which made the gesture all the more meaningful to me. Carolyn was a doer, a planner, a visionary in the staid and placid world of Wichita—but not a counselor, so the spontaneous hug helped thaw the knot of ice in my stomach that had formed back in Dr. Goodnight's office.

As I made my way back to my seat, Shala and Jim both reached out to touch my arm, letting me know they were there if I needed them. Aimee, however, had a better solution. She leaned in, "We're still going to Panera for lunch afterwards, right?" I blinked back tears.

"Of course!" For if Sunday was a time for family and worship, our group knelt at the altar of baked potato soup, tuna on ciabatta bread, and lemonade.

Sunday lunch after service was the only time our entire group could get together in one place. Jim, Shala, Aimee, Luca, Jamey, Jennie, Steve, Susan, and I would drive down to Panera and promptly fill the parking lot. For these people, I could turn even gruesome crime scenes into comedy. For them, I would risk being late to work each Sunday. We weren't the likeliest of friends and family, but the laughter at the table bonded us together rather than the namaste at the end of services.

This was my sacred Sunday ritual. This was the time when Jim would pull out his homemade laser fashioned to look like a Star Trek phaser, or ask if anyone wanted a hellishly strong magnet because he had one in his pocket—I did, and used it to find the screw from my glasses a week later when they broke. The time when Aimee would swish her long blond braid over the back of her chair and accidentally hit an unsuspecting patron behind her. The time when Shala would expound upon her "Christmas stick"—instead of a tree, she and her daughter Luca took a nice fallen branch from the road or a park and decorated it for the holidays. Thus no plants were uprooted and the stick felt useful and pretty. Jamey and Jennie would smile at each other and measure how much larger Jennie's belly had become since last week—their first child, Charlie, was expected in four months—while Steve and Susan would discuss various aspects of work as he struggled to design parts for airplanes and she worked on her guidebook for Wichita. I always wanted to tell her to put Sundays at Panera on the top of her list of places to be in Wichita, but somehow I doubted other people would enjoy it as much as we did. No matter what the mood was before we entered, by the time I left, we had all been laughing for well over forty-five minutes. And I needed that today. My Vagabondian family would support me, of that there was no doubt, but starving artists and bohemians tend to thrive on angst. I would find sympathy there, but not joy nor distractions.

Shala started it that day: "If you have a huge scar on your neck, we can work that into your Halloween costume this year!" she enthused. Aimee backed her up, "I'll help you make it." I picked up the thread, though my eyes still threatened tears.

"You know, one of the treatments is radioactive iodine. I might be radioactive for a while. Maybe I'll get a superpower." Jim's eyes, large and filled with concern only a minute ago, lit up with new thoughts.

"What power?" I shrugged. "Do you get to pick? I thought they just happened." The rest of the conversation flowed around ideas of flying vs. invisibility vs. teleportation. By the time I got to work and told Pat that I'd need a few days off for cancer treatment and surgery, he could only appear somewhat flabbergasted at the cheerful way I broke the news.

"Are you okay?" he asked in concern.

I thought of Dave's hand on my neck, my mom flying out in a few days, Carolyn's arm around me, and the people around a table at Panera. I nodded. "Yeah. I've got a life support system up and running."

CHAPTER ELEVEN
Canine Crimes

I will never buy a dachshund. I know I shouldn't say that, and the anger of the dachshund fanciers community will probably burn my figure in effigy, but dachshunds are evil little dogs. My neighbors Shala and her daughter Luca had a dachshund mix, and every time I went to visit them, the purely malevolent look in her eyes made me cringe. I can handle pit bulls, Doberman Pinschers, and bulldogs, but dachshunds are ... well, they're different. I'm not even sure they're really dogs. I have a theory they're a genetic experiment dreamed up by some evil corporation in an attempt to see if humans will bond with anything that wags its tail, thus building up to their ultimate goal of world domination via tail-wagging robot overlords who mesmerize the masses with their posterior prostheses. This is perhaps not a common view of what Gary Larson always called wiener dogs in his Far Side cartoons, but since I tend to deal with cockroaches, blood, murderers, and sometimes even snakes in the course of my work, I feel one unreasonable phobia and outlandish conspiracy theory is more than acceptable. But my main reason for my aversion—nay, terror—of dachshunds stems from a small kitchen in a tidy little house in one of the poorer suburbs of Wichita.

The call over the radio sounded strange. The officer's voice shook just a little as he reported that he needed a lab investigator. I knew he had been on a death call because they had already called in that it was a code black. In terms of victims, there are those who are code green (fine and dandy), code yellow (need some medical attention, maybe some stitches), code red (get them to an emergency room stat!), code blue (not breathing but maybe they can resuscitate him), and code black (deader than a doornail). There's also a code orange (nutty as a fruitcake) but I didn't generally get called out on those.

I had to learn all this jargon when I started with the Wichita force because if you call out the wrong code at a scene, bad things can happen. Take my coworker, Keith. Keith is a burly fellow and served his Navy time for a number of years before a bad hip and grumpy attitude brought him to Wichita. Or, maybe the grumpy attitude was caused by the bad hip. Lord knows I'm not pleasant to be around when I have a sinus infection, and a constant hip ache must be much, much worse. Keith knew all his ten codes (10-4: I understand, 10-8: leaving the scene, 10-22: arriving on the scene), but he knew a different version of the ten codes. And unbeknownst to most lay people, the ten codes differ between departments. This is a very bad thing, because when police officers transfer departments, or go from federal to state to local positions, they either need to check to make sure their ten codes match the new place, or learn the new ones posthaste. And when a clutch situation arrives, our brains tend to shut off and we revert back to our roots. So an officer in need of backup will call out 10-12, only to have dispatch report that the weather is cloudy with a chance of showers, because he asked for a weather update in his new department. Keith once arrived at a scene, and reported he was, oh, let's say 10-2, meaning he was with the investigating officer, only to have dispatch, in alarm, ask him to repeat himself. He did so, and thought nothing more of it, until sirens started screaming down the pavement toward him because in Wichita, a 10-2 means "engulfed in flames." Keith was the calmest person to ever report he was engulfed in flames in the history of the Wichita police. At least, that was the legend of Keith I was told when I joined the department. I never mustered up the courage to ask him if the legend was based on fact or not.

But the officer of the day was instead reporting that his code black was "suspicious," and that meant hours of work ahead of me as I attempted to pick up every fiber and dust every surface for fingerprints. When I arrived at the scene, the policemen were holding back a crowd. One of the newer officers looked a shade paler than I had ever seen him before. He pulled me into the living room.

"Look, there's something that's not right about this. I've never seen anything like it. I just don't know what to do." This was not good. When the officers come right out and tell you that they're befuddled, and stop hiding behind a macho image of, "I wear a badge and can tell you what to do anytime I damn well please," then you've got problems involving complicated scenes and rather disturbing visuals.

As I edged my way into the kitchen, which I noted was clean with the exception of a single dish on the table that had the remains of a slice of toast with butter and jam, I could see the feet of the deceased. He was lying down, was very thin, and had taken the time to get dressed in nice slacks and brown shoes before sitting down to breakfast. From the photographs of the man and his dog in the living room, I estimated him at about eighty years old. A ripe old age to die, so I figured. At least he'd had a nice long life before he died in a way to make an officer's hands shake while he gave me the details of the call. I stepped around the table for a better look at the body, leapt back, and screamed out "Gah!" in a way that made the officer outside the door turn, smirk, and then call out, "Nothing to see here, folks," in a tone of voice that declared that there was indeed something to see, but they weren't going to get to see it, so they should all go home. Because this man had no face. No eyeballs in the eye sockets, no skin, no nose, no lips or chin. It was all gone, down to the fat layer of the cheek pads.

I edged back around the table and took a closer look. The hands were intact, and the officer told me that this man had been seen just that morning at 6 a.m. It was only four in the afternoon now and though it was hot in the building, there were no signs of insects or decomposition yet. He was just starting to go into rigor mortis. I looked about wildly as if somehow his face had jumped off his head and was now perched jauntily on the countertop. I mean, where had it gone? Had someone skinned this poor man? He lived in a very modest house, which was quite clean, and his neighbors testified that they had never seen him without his fedora, even if he was just walking to the mailbox to pick up the mail. Just a lovely old gentleman living quietly in his retirement years in the same two-bedroom house where he and his wife had raised two children. Where had his face gone? Who had taken it? Did we have some deranged person on the loose who skinned people's faces?

I took a couple of deep breaths and went back out to the living room.

"Were the doors locked when you arrived?" I asked the officer.

He nodded. But the neighbors had heard the dog whining and the man had been sick recently, so they were concerned and called for a welfare check. And there he was, the man without a face. I told the officer to check with the neighbors and family and find out who this man's doctor was. I didn't know what flesh-eating bacteria did, and I didn't think it would dissolve someone's face, but I'm not a doctor and maybe there was a face-dissolving bacteria on the loose in Wichita.

I took my camera in hand and went back to the kitchen to start my photographs, and said "Oh, LORD!!" because there was no face-dissolving bacteria on the loose in Wichita. Nor was there a face-skinning maniac rampaging through the streets. But there was a dachshund in the house. A morbidly obese dachshund who was currently tearing at the fat layer of the dead man's cheeks with his teeth and clearly enjoying the meal.

"Stop! Scat! Get away!" I screamed out and he went over to cower in the corner. As my gaze went around the room, I couldn't help but notice—"Oh, for god's sake! You still have dog food in your bowl! You ate his face when you still had food in your bowl? Jesus!" I stumbled backward over a kitchen chair and into the living room.

"Hey, Jason," I called out to the officer, "any word yet from the guy's doctor?"

Jason nodded. He was writing in his pad as dispatch blared over his radio.

"Yeah, I'm on a private channel, go ahead."

I could hear the voice of the dispatch person from my position across the room, which meant that Megan was on duty today. She had a shrill enough voice to break glass at a thousand miles (at least over the radio).

"Victim's doctor saw him yesterday for his heart condition. He said he'd sign a death certificate cause the guy's ticker was really bad," Megan reported to Jason and the rest of the western hemisphere. Jason nodded, and then gulped.

"Hey, Megan, did he say anything about the guy's face…?" He trailed off as I frantically waved my arms. No one needed to hear Megan shriek out that someone's face was missing, especially since it had just been relocated to the stomach of an obese dachshund.

"Uh, never mind." Jason clicked off and I relayed what I had seen. "Holy shit, the dog ate his face?" Jason asked.

I nodded. "And with a doctor to sign off, we don't need to be here except for one person to wait for the mortuary," I explained.

Jason looked worried. "Hey, Laura, where's the dog now?"

I gasped. I had left the dog in the kitchen with the dead man. Unguarded.

We raced back into the next room and I breathed a sigh of relief. The dog was still in the corner where I had shooed him, looking at us with sad soulful eyes. Eyes that said, "Pity me, I just lost my owner and I need someone to love me." Eyes that betrayed no hint of the next sentence, "I also ate my owner's face for reasons I cannot fully explain at this time."

Jason grabbed the dog's collar and thrust him outside the kitchen door into the fenced-in yard. He closed the door quickly and with an, "And stay out!"

We sat down next to the faceless man to wait for the mortuary van. And I couldn't help snapping a few pictures just for my own memories. Oh, I wouldn't use names or addresses, but one day in the distant future, when I was a professor of forensic science at some local college in my retirement years, I would put this slide up and ask my students, "So what happened to his face? Is this a suspicious death scene to you?" and then tell them about the evils of dachshunds.

We went outside to greet the mortuary van and representative and to tell him that this would most likely be a closed-casket funeral. As we rounded the corner, the man's son came running up.

"I heard about my dad. We knew he didn't have long. Is... everything all right? Why is the crime van here?" I told him that it was just a precaution we took if we couldn't immediately get ahold of the deceased's medical professional, but that no crime had been committed, and we turned to go.

"Hey, Barry! That's a good boy!" I heard the man's son say. I turned and watched him (in slow motion, or so it seemed) pick up the dog, who began to enthusiastically wag its tail and lick his face—and I couldn't stop shuddering for the rest of the day.

CHAPTER TWELVE
The Day No One Died

I pulled up to the Motel 6 and experienced an odd sense of déjà vu. Actually, I suppose it wasn't so odd, seeing as how I had stayed there a mere two months ago when I had flown out for my interview with the crime lab. Having just gotten out of graduate school, I didn't have the money for a fancy luxury like the Holiday Inn, but the Motel 6 was just my speed. The $17-a-night room for one night had been clean, and had a bed, and really, that was all I needed at the time.

But now the reds and blues of police lights strobed through the sky. I felt just a twinge of triumph because this was the first scene I had ever found, on my own, without consulting the giant map of the city on the crime lab wall, or getting lost and calling in over the radio for directions. Somehow, I seem to create a "sense of direction vortex" about me, no matter where I go. It works like a charm if you ever need to get lost, because no matter where I am, no matter how many times I've been there before, I and everyone around me will inevitably lose our way, only to have me realize approximately twelve minutes later that I've been lost there before. And then I find my way out by the same roundabout route I used the last time I had been lost in that particular spot. Those people around me who always claimed to have an excellent sense of direction would generally lose their way, as well. And, if heaven forbid I ever stopped for directions at a gas station, the station attendant, who had been born, grown up, gotten married, and worked there for the past thirty years would suddenly find himself scratching his head and saying, "Milford Street? Well, now let me think," followed by a panicked look as he suddenly realized that he not only had no idea where Milford Street was, even though his best friend of forty years had lived there and he had just had dinner there last night, but Milford Street had suddenly vanished off his internal map of the city forever. Indeed, I had once been lost on a straight road with no turn-offs and had to pull over and study a map for thirty minutes before I discovered that the road had merely changed names from one end of the city to the other and I had been a block from the scene the entire time. But this time around I had not gotten lost. I had not gotten lost in part because I had been there before, but mostly because there was only one highway that ran in the east/west direction of the city and if you just drove west on it long enough, you'd find yourself at the Motel 6.

All the homicide detectives were clustered around outside the building, and all of them wore somber expressions. I had never seen one of them smile, except in a sad, self-deprecating way, as if their jobs had removed all the humor from their systems. I understood. It's extremely difficult to see the things homicide detectives look at day after day and maintain any sense of equilibrium. Even I had good days when my only call would be a burglary at a pet store, where someone took five dollars' worth of flea shampoo and I'd spend the first thirty minutes of my "investigation" playing with a puppy that looked like the cute one from the Cottonelle toilet paper commercials, only cuddlier. But homicide detectives never get a break from death. They interview people about the dead person. They work crime scenes only involving dead people. They follow an elusive paper trail that we leave behind when we die, composed of sales receipts, credit card statements, and magazine subscriptions. Everything about their job reeks of death every day, and if that doesn't take the joy out of your eyes, then you're a more well-adjusted person than most.

Every police officer wants to be a homicide detective because that's the pinnacle of detective work, and the status and prestige that are accorded to them outrank any other job on the force. Of course, along with the prestige comes the crushing weight of cases that never leave your thoughts for a moment. The head of the department was haunted by a spate of homicides that had taken place over twenty years ago but had never been solved. He had worked on those as a junior homicide detective, and the lack of resolution wore him down until his skin was as thin as the pages of those case files that still sat on his desk. He had perfected a world-weary slump and the dedicated glint in his eye. If you had him working on a case, you could tell at one glance that he would never let it go until he could give you all the answers you so desperately wanted.

Today, he looked angry. "The damn thing just doesn't make any sense!" he barked at me. I paused in mid-stride. All I had been prepared to ask was if he had a case number for me to reference in my report, but… that could wait. I turned to the detective next to me.

"Want to show me which room?" I asked him. He nodded and slouched up the outdoor staircase to the second floor. Drat. I hate second floor scenes, because it means carrying so much equipment up the stairs. It isn't that I'm too weak to do it, but it just takes time, and once in a scene, I don't like to have to leave it to get equipment that I need. Plus, if it's a homicide scene, you have to wear booties to avoid transferring the dirt and detritus on the bottom of your shoes to the floor of the scene. And each time you leave a scene, you've got to change booties. Since I'm about as graceful as a penguin on land, this usually involves me falling down at least once. The agents on CSI never fall down when they put their booties on. Then again, they don't wear booties over their high-heeled shoes. Personally, I prefer sturdy closed-toed boots when I'm at a scene, since sometimes it involves walking around and through various bodily fluids.

The detective showed me into a typical Motel 6 room, identical to the one I had stayed in just a few weeks before. Bed. Small dresser. Nightstand. Closet. Bathroom. TV. That was it. Aside from the blood. It was rather hard to miss the blood. There was a smear of it on the wall, about head height, going horizontally for about three feet. A small pool of blood on the fitted sheet on the bed glared reddish-brown in contrast to the off-white color that too many washings had given the bedding. A small bag of toiletries on the nightstand contained deodorant, a razor, and a bar of soap. A black wallet on the nightstand caught my eye, as did the set of car keys next to it. That's never good, I thought. People tend to take those sorts of things with them when they check out of motels. I know I always do. We walked across to the bathroom where the detective showed me two small drops of blood on the shower floor. As we came back to the room, I noticed a suitcase lying between the bed and the closet, and for the first time realized that there was no top sheet on the bed— only the fitted sheet and a blanket.

"Is that it?" I asked. He nodded and left me to get to work. I started with photographs. Photographs of every angle of the room, overall, mid-range, and close-up shots of various items I'd be collecting, but without moving anything. I'd photograph it again when I moved it. I sketched out the area, thankful that it was just one room and a bathroom, with very little furniture. I quickly made boxes on the graph paper to indicate the bed, nightstand, and TV, cleverly labeled as "bed," "nightstand," and "TV." But then again, I never claimed to be da Vinci.

Measuring a room is one of the hardest tasks at a scene if you're working by yourself. The tape measure is always blocked by furniture, and if you take too many measurements at one time before writing them down, you'll forget them all. But if you stop and write down the numbers after each measurement, it'll take you twice as long to finish up and get out to the next call. Motel 6 rooms are great in such circumstances because there's very little to get in the way. Put in a standard thirty-six inch door and you're basically set.

I went through the wallet and found the owner's driver's license, credit cards, and Blockbuster video membership card. No cash, though. There was nothing else in the bag of toiletries and nothing in the nightstand other than a note that the Gideons had been there and left a Bible behind. I checked through it just to be sure nothing was written inside that might be important to the case, only to hear the spine crack when I opened it. Clearly, Motel 6 patrons were not Bible-reading types. As I made my way on hands and knees to the bed, all the while doing tape lifts of the carpet in a grid pattern and sliding the tapes into their own separate plastic bags, I kept turning the blood stain on the wall over and over in my mind. There was something wrong about it. The head of the homicide unit was right. But keeping to a specific order is important in a scene, and the bed was next in line. I photographed the bloodstain on the sheet again and then took a closer look. With one gloved hand I pulled on the sheet and a small slit, about two inches wide in the middle of the bloodstain, opened up. Something had been stabbed through the sheet. Stabbed through the sheet, and as I removed it I saw the same size slit in the mattress that went fairly far down. I took out my utility knife and cut out the damaged part of the mattress. By looking at it, it seemed to be about four inches deep, but a measurement at the lab would tell me for sure.

I turned my attention to the blood on the wall and frowned. It just didn't add up. One smear about three feet long and with clear finger trails through it. It was as if someone had blood on his hand and had just swiped it once along the wall. But there was no spatter anywhere in the room. If someone had been stabbed, there should be blood spatter somewhere. On the wall behind the bed, on the floor, on the wall with the smear, on the ceiling. Somewhere, there should be droplets of blood. The two drops of blood in the shower on the floor were perfectly round. They had dropped straight down and no water had been run over them. The shower was dry. If you washed yourself off, the blood should be streaked, if it's left there at all. This whole scene looked as if someone had watched a couple of episodes of Law & Order and then attempted to fake a scene. I was reminded of the practical exams I'd had in grad school where my instructors would create fake scenes for us to process. The UV light gave me no further insight and without any spatter to string, I couldn't say how many blows to the person there had been or where they had been in the room when it happened, or at what velocity the spatter was traveling when it reached the wall. I sighed and packed up my kit. It just didn't add up.

The head of homicide was waiting for me downstairs with a case number and the details of the scene history. Generally, I get those before I process a scene, but I was still a little scared of him, and he hadn't been in a good mood when I arrived. I briefed him on my findings and agreed with his assessment.

"It doesn't add up," I told him. "There's no spatter and if someone had been stabbed in the bed, and dragged out in the sheet, then you'd need a knife the size of a machete to go that far into a mattress if it goes through the whole human body first. There wasn't any water in the shower… It just looks wrong."

He nodded and sighed. Mysteries belong on PBS, not here. We got into our respective cars and drove away.

The following week more details emerged. The missing person had been heavily indebted to some rather menacing fellows in town who ran the dog tracks. His wife was filing for divorce and was requesting alimony in exorbitant amounts. His credit cards were maxed out and people were calling, trying to collect. And then two weeks after the scene, there was a break in the case—a rather large break. The missing man had been arrested in Missouri for punching a police officer during a bar fight. Seems he decided to fake his death to get away from his creditors and wife and start life over again in a new state. Of course, if you're starting life over and you're on the run from "the man," most people would find it best to not start a fight with "the man." But that's most people. As it was, he was alive, well, and in jail. The head of homicide smiled at me. For once, he'd had a case where no one died.

CHAPTER THIRTEEN

Order In the Court

I should probably have worn my uniform instead of a suit. I should have had my hair done professionally. I should have put on a little less lipstick and a little more eyeliner. But at least I was wearing my glasses. I needed to look smart and everyone knows that girls who wear glasses are smart. (That's why boys in high school tend not to ask us out.) I was going to lean back in the chair and tip over while everyone watched. I just knew it. Katie Neith had done that at my birthday party in the fifth grade. She had jumped into our rocking chair and it just tipped on over. (It was a very old rocking chair and was used to more gentle treatment.) And now I was going to do it in front of a judge, jury, and executioner. Well, perhaps not an executioner. This wasn't a capital murder case after all. But it was a marital rape case, and the fact that it had even made it to court was a triumph that no one, not one lab person, not one detective, and certainly not the prosecutor, had ever expected.

Marital rape and domestic violence cases rarely go to court, because the victims generally back out of testifying. And I can't say I blame them. They have long histories with the perpetrators, and the violence of the crime is mitigated by the love they feel, and of course, the suspects generally go through a cycle where they apologize and attempt to make up for their past actions. And no victim wants to go up on the stand and tell twelve strangers, an audience, and a man in a black toga that her marriage has failed. That she's scared of the person she married and promised to love in good times and in bad. Because this is the Midwest, with its traditional philosophy of marriage.

My best friend (the friendly officer from my first burglary) happens to be one of the most impressive women I've ever met. She was a mere 23 years old and had already gotten her college degree, graduated from the police academy, and purchased a house, and she was incredibly beautiful to boot. Yet she considered herself a failure because she wasn't married. I had attempted on numerous occasions to instill a little East Coast philosophy of "marriage should wait until you're thirty-five anyway because then you'll know your own mind and be better able to merge your life with another person's," but with little success.

On weekends we would go to one of the local meat markets so that she could hopefully find husband material. I hated those places, but she was my friend and besides, this way I could keep an eye on her and make sure no one slipped anything extra into her drinks. Having spent the last few years either in classes called "Medico-Legal Investigations of Death" or working on crime scenes, I found myself expecting the worst of the local male population. So domestic violence victims quietly draw their tattered dignity about them, explain to the hospital workers, police, and crime scene investigators that they really are fine and that they provoked their spouses into punching them, and really it didn't hurt that much and it looked much worse than it was, and walked on home after refusing to sign a complaint. And always, they started their walk with hunched shoulders and then about five paces into the walk up to the front door, they would pause and straighten them. Because the neighbors and the children needed to see them walk in without a defeated posture. Every damn time.

So it was with complete shock that I had answered the telephone in the lab one day to hear a prosecutor tell me, "We'll need you in court on Monday for the Dobson case." The Dobson case? I couldn't even remember which case that was. Because another thing they don't mention on TV is how long it takes for cases to get to trial. I had worked the rape scene at the Dobson residence eight months earlier, and it was only now getting to the courtroom. And that was a rather quick result. Usually the paper summonses to court would come in, and I would look at them and toss them aside, knowing full well that things would plead out, or get dismissed, or be tossed on technicalities. I had been in Wichita for ten months and had yet to appear in court.

I scrambled for my old field notebook and looked up my notes for Dobson. They had been going through a trial separation, and he had been staying somewhere else, while she lived in the house. That evening, he had come in the back door, taken a knife from the kitchen, grabbed her by her hair, and dragged her into the bedroom, where he raped her. He held the knife to her throat the whole time. After he had gotten up and pulled up his trousers, he dropped the knife and headed out. She kicked the knife under the bed so that if he came back, he wouldn't be able to get to it again, and then she called the police. She had no bruises, because she hadn't fought him—and with a knife to her neck, who could fault her for that?

DNA was useless because he had just left the house a couple of days ago and the sheets on the bed hadn't been changed yet. Of course we'd find his DNA on his sheets. If she hadn't kicked the knife under the bed, this case would not have been in court. But it was there under the bed. I had lifted up the corner of the sheet, peered into the gloom, and seen the glint of the metal. The handle was a rough material that wouldn't be good for fingerprints. The only piece of evidence to back up her story was the location of the knife itself. He of course claimed that their sexual intercourse was consensual and that she probably now regretted it because he had told her that he wasn't coming back home. I would need to testify about the knife and about the photographs I'd taken and the sketch I'd done at the scene.

The defense attorney was not a happy man. There wasn't much he could challenge on this case, and to top it all off, the air conditioner wasn't working in the courtroom, and he was in a full suit, as was his client. Very few rape cases involved weapons, and even fewer hinged on the lone fact of that weapon's location within a house. It was just his bad luck that his client hadn't taken the knife with him and put it back in the kitchen as he left the house. He glared at me.

"CSI Merz," he intoned. "This is the very first time you've ever been in a courtroom, isn't that right?"

"Yes," I answered.

"Your Honor, I move to strike this witness and her testimony. She is clearly new to the job and not an expert in the field of crime scenes."

Prosecution jumped up.

"Your Honor, CSI Merz is here to testify as to what she observed at the scene and her actions there. She is not being presented as an expert."

Though I knew he was merely trying to get my testimony in, and to win the case, I felt betrayed. I was an expert, damn it. I was very good at my job, had a degree in the field, and knew far more about crime scenes than those so-called CSIs on TV. But my feelings weren't the point. The point was to win the case. The point was to put a man who raped a woman in jail. My feelings did not matter.

Breathe, I told myself, and don't tilt back in the chair.

"The court will allow the witness."

"CSI Merz, you said you found this knife, Exhibit A, in the bedroom under the bed, but yet you cannot say if it was placed there by the suspect or the victim, and you don't know when it got there, and even if you did know who put it there, you wouldn't know a time frame, and if you knew the time frame, that wouldn't tell you who put it there, isn't that true? Please answer yes or no."

I had tried to concentrate on the question, really I had, but there was no way I could answer yes or no without explaining which part was yes, and which was no. I had been warned that defense attorneys liked to play these sorts of tricks, especially if they had a weak case.

"I'm sorry, could you rephrase that?" I asked.

Defense glared again. "If you could say who put that knife there, and if you knew when it was there, that wouldn't tell you one part if you only knew the other part, isn't that right? Yes or no?"

I felt my throat begin to close up and panic hit. "I'm sorry. I didn't follow the question. Could you simplify it?"

By now the defense attorney was on his feet and waving his arms. "Your Honor, I move this witness be disqualified and her testimony stricken and this evidence be thrown out. She obviously cannot follow any of my questions about it!"

The judge, a good old boy from the Midwest, a cowboy who probably would rather deal with cattle than with criminals, heaved a sigh.

"Mr. Jones," he sighed again and shifted in his seat. "Bloodhounds couldn't follow that question. Now you ask 'em the right way, or you sit yourself down."

Silence fell. In the quiet, juror number three suddenly snorted into her notebook. Juror seven followed while lucky number thirteen, the alternate, hid his face in his hands as his shoulders shook. Prosecution's mouth twitched, and finally a wave of laughter overtook the observers.

For the love of god, don't laugh, I told myself. Do not laugh. You are on the witness stand. Maintain your professionalism and do not laugh. Or tilt the chair back. Do not laugh or tilt.

The judge banged his gavel. "I appreciate you know a good line when you hear one, but you all quiet down." Defense deflated and asked me only two short questions:

"You can't say when the knife was put under the bed, can you?"

"No, I cannot."

"You can't say who put the knife there, can you?"

"No, I cannot."

"No further questions, Your Honor."

The judge dismissed me and I was free to go. It took the jury only forty-five minutes to come back with a guilty verdict. Even the prosecutor looked surprised, and that, I thought to myself, just shouldn't be so.

The bed sheet had blood on it. Smudges, dots, and smears. It wasn't a lot of blood if you took it by volume, but then again, in consensual sex, how much blood is generally left on the sheet? Two tiny drops of blood spatter dotted the wall by the pillows. It was all I saw initially, so after I took my photographs, I got out my flashlight and turned off the lights.

I always hated it on the CSI shows when the investigators searched a scene in the dark. How could they see anything? Why didn't they just TURN ON THE LIGHT? I would scream at my television. But when you're looking for trace evidence, it's best to turn off the light and sweep the flashlight beam low over the ground, almost skimming the carpet with the body of the flashlight so that any hairs or small pieces of debris create shadows. I collected several long hairs from the floor and noted their roots were intact. Though we shed over one hundred hairs a day, we don't shed the roots. Roots appear when hairs are plucked or pulled out of the head. Roots on hairs at crime scenes indicate force was used. The blood turned black against the UV light, but I was on the prowl for other bodily fluids. Semen and vaginal fluid appeared to be present and were verified by a field test of acid phosphatase. The swab of the glowing stain turned pink as I watched.

One of the pillows seemed to have much more saliva on it than I normally saw. It might have been an old stain, but when I looked at it under normal lighting, I realized it was still damp. Shoved in her mouth perhaps? Did she bite it in pleasure or pain? The stain wouldn't say, and I lacked Gil Grissom's crime scene flashback ability. But I would collect the pillow. The two dots of blood on the wall surprised me. They were spatter and they were fresh. Spatter indicates a blow of some kind. Spatter indicates force.

CHAPTER FOURTEEN
Darwin Awards

I'm generally not a huge fan of awards shows. Every year a bunch of people get together and try to tell us which movies are the best and brightest, though at least they seem to care about movie quality rather than box office revenues, which gives me some hope for Hollywood, though not a whole lot. I think the Oscars tend to make normal people lose their minds. My college roommate once was paid quite a nice sum of money to dress up in a gold bodysuit and ice skate on a glycerin-covered balcony outside a high-rise apartment building during the tenant's Oscar party to create the right "ambiance."

But there's one awards list that I wait for every year with bated breath. One awards list that can make me stop whatever it is I'm doing, go out, and buy the book. I speak of course of the Darwin Awards. Those wonderful men and women who, through their own stupidity, have managed to take themselves out of the gene pool. While my roommate was being paid by delusional wealthy people to be their living, ice-skating Oscar statue, I was studying anthropology, where we discussed the eugenics movement at great length. There were government programs in a number of countries from the 1920s to the 1940s in which scientists and politicians got together and decided who had the right to procreate and who did not. And those deemed unworthy were forcibly sterilized, or killed, depending on the country. And this was bad. We can generally all agree that the government peons in most countries probably don't have, shall we say, the nuanced grasp of science and ethics to make these sorts of decisions. So I'm against the government meddling with reproductive issues, but if people wish to remove themselves from the gene pool, I'm quite happy to let them.

The call came in around 9 p.m. The lab at the hospital needed photographs taken of injuries. These are some of the easiest calls, since there's very little else to do besides snapping a couple of pictures and taking a case history. Usually the doctor has been given permission by the patient to disclose the source of the injury and after jotting down a few notes, I take my pictures and head back to the lab. These calls can either come in from the hospital itself, because the victim has voluntarily come in for treatment, or from the police department because they have to transport a victim from a scene to the hospital for medical aid. It had been a quiet evening, and I didn't recall any officers going out to scenes and reporting injuries to anyone, which meant that the victim had come into the hospital on his or her own, so I speculated. I preferred those sorts of calls because that meant the injuries probably weren't life-threatening. As I walked down the hallway at the hospital, I noticed something different about the hushed whispers that generally accompanied the medical conversations between the nurses and doctors. I could have sworn I heard muffled laughter. After the fifth person ducked behind a desk when I passed by, I started to become self-conscious. Was my uniform on wrong? Had my pants zipper come down unexpectedly? Did I have a cloud of black powder around my nose from the last place I had fingerprinted? (A short side note about fingerprint powder: Black powder is very fine and is impossible to get rid of. As you dust for fingerprints, you will inhale a bit of it. It's a harmless substance, but if you are not warned, the first time you blow your nose after a scene and you see all these black flecks on the tissue, you will panic. Patti tells me that after one particularly dusty scene, I sneezed and a cloud of black powder came out my nose. That never happens to Grissom.) After a detour to the bathroom mirror where I saw no sign of uniform mishaps or powdery problems, I continued to the emergency room. The nurse who I thought looked just like Carol from the TV show ER (if Carol had had blond hair) saw me coming and quickly pulled me aside.

"Do you know about this case?" she asked.

"Non-life-threatening injuries?" I queried.

Carol II nodded. "Well… yes. That's true. But they are rather unusual injuries. He's burned pretty badly."

I winced.

Burns are the worst injuries to photograph. The person is usually in extreme pain, and depending on the severity of the burn, the skin can split, or can be burned away all together. Sometimes the fat layer of the human body is exposed. And usually burn victims are children.

Oh, sometimes they are adults who have been caught in a fire, but I had never seen one of those. I had, however seen many children who had been scalded by boiling water or other liquids. I had heard their cries and watched the nurses and possibly their parents try to soothe them. Sometimes it was determined that it really was just an accident. A curious four-year-old who pulled the spaghetti pot down off the stove because he was hungry and he could finally reach the top. Or a two-year-old who just got underfoot as her mother turned to take the pot off the stove and drain the pasta. She tripped and suddenly dinner was cancelled in favor of a trip to the emergency room. But sometimes burns were deliberate. And sometimes the parents lied about it. You could generally tell if the hospital suspected abuse by the way the people in the background talked and looked at the parent giving the police report. If they muttered and looked down or glared, or looked at the room where the child was, then they suspected something wasn't quite right. If they looked at the parent in sympathy, if they offered him or her a chair or a glass of water, interrupting the interview, then you had a pretty good idea that the injuries matched up with the history given by the parent.

One hysterical mother could barely speak between sobs as she relayed how she had stepped on her son's toy car and just went down, getting the boiling water all over her son as he sat in his high chair. The police officer was dutifully taking notes, but as I watched the hospital staff, I saw one of them finally shrug in disgust and stalk away into the child's room. I hadn't seen the victim yet, and this seemed a good time to take my photographs and also satisfy my curiosity. It wasn't my place to interview anyone, but if there was anything I needed to know for my photographs I was allowed to ask.

"Something up?" We always whisper in the rooms of victims. Even if they can't understand a word we say, we still do it. The nurse turned to me.

"He was sitting in his high chair, and she spilled water on him."

I nodded. That was the story.

"Then explain to me how the bottoms of his feet got the worst of the burns."

Uh-oh. Were the hysterics remorse? Were they out of fear of being caught? Were they an act? I never did find out. I just took the pictures and let the detectives worry about solving the case.

So when Carol II mentioned burns, I paled and stopped mid-stride.

I can photograph most injuries. I have to prepare for burns.

"No, no. Nothing like that." Carol pulled me to the side of the doorway. "Do you know how to make meth?"

I may be master of the non sequitur but even I had to think about how this fit in. "Not really."

Carol nodded. "They were trying to make meth," she explained. "And they needed anhydrous ammonia." As it turned out, these two boys, who were not, shall we say, mental giants, were attempting to make meth and had gathered the necessary ingredients, with the exception of anhydrous ammonia (which is used by farmers for soil treatments). Wichita has a lot of farms that have ammonia tanks that can be tapped to fertilize the fields. Of course, they're kept under strict pressure and temperature controls because this is a nasty chemical. It boils at minus thirty-three degrees Celsius and causes chemical burns when it comes in contact with the skin. The anhydrous part of the name means that there's no water in this chemical, so it will basically react to anything that has water in it. It will suck out the moisture and boil itself into a gas, which is its normal state of being under regular temperatures and pressures. These two geniuses had taken this chemical and put it in an old metal chemical container they had pilfered from an older farm for transport. They'd loaded it up on the back of their pickup truck and then, to keep the lid closed, one of them had sat on it, while the other drove the truck. And this had placed male genitals perilously close to very bad chemicals, and yes, the inevitable happened. As they were bouncing across the farmer's field, in their pickup truck, swerving about in their excitement over obtaining the last ingredient they needed to make their drug of choice, boy number two fell back off the container and managed to spill anhydrous ammonia all over his lap. The chemical began to react immediately with the air, his pants, and his skin, and before you knew it, this boy had managed to chemically separate himself from his genitals. Or nearly had. His buddy, hearing the screams, stopped the truck and ran out to see what had happened. He panicked and drove straight to the hospital, which is when they made the call to us. Carol stopped and looked at me. Ah. Oh. Oh, lord. "He burned it off?" I asked. Carol nodded. "We had to remove some of the damaged tissue. There's… not much left."

I should not giggle at times like these. This was a serious matter. There was a young man who was badly hurt in that room. And while yes, he did cause his injuries, I would not have been laughing if he had accidentally shot himself while he was cleaning a gun. I should not laugh. I definitely should not laugh. Unfortunately, when I say this, I always hear my father's voice saying in a deep and serious manner, "Don't laugh." He would say this to me when I was upset and repeat it, with increasing austerity. And I would always break down and laugh. Always. I would try to hold onto my anger but I could feel it slipping away. Whatever teen crisis was causing my ire would somehow leave my consciousness as I focused on not laughing rather than on the trials and tribulations of the day. And once my focus shifted to not laughing, I could never stop the laughter. So Carol and I barely made it to the bathroom before we broke. As we leaned on each other, gasping, panting for air, Carol wiped her eyes.

"We really shouldn't laugh."

"I know. But oh lord. How stupid could you be?" Carol nodded.

"Is he awake?" I asked. "No. We thought it best to keep him sedated."

We made our way back to the victim's room and walked in. He was wearing a plain hospital gown and looked painfully thin, as most meth addicts did if they'd been at it for a while. I'm always amazed that people who barely have enough brain function to speak can figure out not only how to make meth, but also manage to build a lab, get the materials, and actually follow through with the plan. Carol pulled back his gown and indicated the area of injury, though really, I could see for myself where the damage was. It was rather obvious, after all. I took the photographs, which were evidence of his guilt in the theft of anhydrous ammonia, and stepped back. He would live. He might even kick the meth habit after this, though I doubted it. He would probably need the drug even more now to forget just how badly he injured himself. And he would never procreate. My Darwin Award winner, who had probably inhabited the shallow end of the gene pool for most of his life, had finally gotten himself out of it altogether. And better yet, lived to tell the tale.

CHAPTER FIFTEEN
Small Ugly Boats

In truth, I couldn't remember who gave me the wand. I knew Luca brought the sparkly headband with two clover leaves on small springs that bobbled whenever I moved my head, glitter spelling out "happy" on one and "b-day" on the other, that currently sat atop my head. I knew the Vagabond staff kindly looked the other way when Luca and Shala showed up—Luca being not of legal drinking age yet—because we assured them the strongest drink consumed would be chai tea or coffee, plus Shala was Luca's mom and Luca wouldn't drink alcohol in front of her, plus it was my twenty-fifth birthday and therefore exceptions would just have to be made. I knew Jim had his laser out and was making various crystal knick-knacks light up with a green sparkling glow, Jamey and Jennie had brought the cake, Heather had brought a bemused smile on her face as this was her first interaction with both the Unitarians and the Vagabondians (luckily, Heather was adaptable to all situations), but who on earth had brought the birthday wand? It was up to me to decree the rules of the evening. We were in the midst of a cutthroat game of go-fish Scrabble—a game akin to my other creation of communist poker (where if someone goes out, you just redistribute the wealth so everyone can keep playing). The rules were simple—make the best word you could, but if you needed a letter, say to make a really good word such as "paucity" but you lacked the "u," well then you got to ask someone if they had that letter and if so, they could give it to you. You were also allowed to go off the actual board if you needed more space. It was about word creation and creativity rather than limiting your imagination to the confines of the board. Though a few objections arose, I pointed out that it was my birthday—PLUS, I had a wand. In the face of such indisputable facts, arguing was futile.

Earlier in the evening, Shala had successfully acted out the word "hormone" in a game of Cranium, and Jim had presented me with what can probably be called the best use of an AOL CD ever. Etched into the silver side of the CD, tiny points and lines connecting them made up the constellations. Jim clearly still retained hope that I might one day learn more about constellations than my usual standbys of Orion and the Big Dipper. We had gone out into the wilds of Kansas on more than one occasion with his homemade telescope as he tried to point out such astronomical oddities as "Leo."

"See," he would tell me, "there up to your left? That's the curve of Leo's mane. And if you follow that on a straight line over that way, you'll see Gemini."

I would nod gamely and enthusiastically, while knowing quite well that never again would I find the curve of Leo's mane. Aimee and I had also engaged in several rooftop stargazing trips with Jim at his house, but sadly, despite his best efforts, I remained firmly earthbound. Still, I loved those sessions, feeling the gritty roof tiles beneath my hands and feet, lying on our backs staring up into space, as the conversation meandered from Venus to Roman gods to Audrey Hepburn (via the movie Roman Holiday). Jim's CD most likely wouldn't help me locate any of the constellations in the actual night sky, but securely armed with it, I would always be able to point to Leo. "See," I would be able to say, "it's right here on the disc!"

For the fourth time that night, Pete and Cate informed someone that the back room was reserved for a private party. They came in every so often to check on who needed refills of chai or to sneak a piece of birthday cake. We had smuggled it in, so to speak, if you extend the definition of smuggling to include walking in with the cake in plain sight and asking the proprietor if it was all right to smuggle this cake into the building. But because of the smuggled cake, we weren't ordering any food, and I knew they were losing money by keeping the back room off limits to anyone not involved with my birthday. I vowed to leave a really exorbitant tip when I left. My bill being all of seven dollars for multiple teas, a ten-dollar tip might seem ridiculous, but they'd know why I left it. I also resolved to come up with some fresh crime scene stories even if it meant taking calls when I wasn't next on the rotation. I looked longingly after Pete as he left the room. My crush on him hadn't faded after the acid phosphatase competition as I had expected, but so far, I hadn't made any progress on that front. Shala was quick to point out that it was hard to make progress when I refused to (a) tell him I liked him, (b) ask him out, or (c) at least flirt with him a little. I rebutted that with the fact that it was difficult to do any of those things when one was still recovering from surgery and had a giant red scar on her neck. We had, however, figured out that my Halloween costume would involve a scenario with a severed and reattached head, which would be all the more believable due to the presence of a real scar. The tumors had been contained within my thyroid, and after surgery I had been given a clean bill of health, which relieved everyone. This was my first big celebration since the surgery, and we were making the most of it. Luca snapped a picture of me in mid-laugh and passed the camera on. Jim smiled. "You've got the same look as on New Year's. I think you're recovered."

I had been extremely lucky with holidays in my first year in Wichita. Although my "weekend" fell on Wednesdays and Thursdays, as luck would have it, Christmas, New Year's, and my birthday all fell on my weekends. And although a trip to New Orleans with my college friends for Christmas lightened the holiday mood for me, New Year's had loomed with no plans, no date, and no one with whom I could count down as the ball dropped. Jim came to the rescue when he told me that he would be happy if I showed up at a party that would include Carolyn's son and several other Unitarians with whom I had a passing friendship. I was still a little shy around Jim since he was twenty years older than I was, but I jumped at the chance to be with people to ring in the New Year rather than counting down alone in my apartment. Jim was known as "Mr. Science" to those of us in church and always had a project to work on. The hole in his garage door that had been caused by a tomato traveling at high velocity out of his experimental tomato gun was the stuff of Wichita legend. I had volunteered my services as an apprentice to him, though we had not started on any of his ideas. (He had found instructions online for the building of a small ugly boat, which concerned me, since the vessel seemed destined to be named with the acronym "sub.") But most importantly, Jim had the kindest soul of any person I had ever met. There were times I envied his wife and hoped that one day, I'd meet someone my age who had his sensibilities. For any crisis that arose, I knew that if there were no female friends around to comfort me, Jim would be just as good as, if not better than those blessed with a double X chromosome. We had been at the New Year's party for about an hour when we made our way out of the house and into the backyard toward the bonfire. For the first time I could remember, my New Year would not start with a glowing ball in Times Square.

Instead, we had a huge bonfire and a trampoline—though the trampoline was nowhere near the fire. Unitarians may be eccentric but we're fully aware of personal safety. Jim, another girl I hadn't met, and I clambered onto the trampoline and started to jump. We held hands and leapt toward the stars, laughing at the childhood memories and sheer joy of being a little less tied to the earth.

I smiled at Jim across the table at the Vagabond. "Yeah, I think I'm recovered. Oh and hey, have you ever thought about renaming the Small Ugly Boat?"

CHAPTER SIXTEEN
The CSI Effect

Fingerprints are elusive, invisible, easily smudged or destroyed, and utterly infuriating. They can be processed with superglue fuming and dye stain, ninhydrin, liquids, and powders. They can be lifted with regular tape, thick tapes, gel lifts, glue, microsil, or not lifted at all. Sometimes you just have to photograph them with black and white film on a 1:1 ratio and use that image as your evidence. For years, they have been the standard of identification and the staple of crime scenes. Of course, now DNA is the new bright and shining star, but unless the suspect happens to bleed, spit, or leave a part of his skin behind at a scene, advances in DNA aren't helpful. DNA also takes time and laboratory work to identify, and in Wichita, that meant sending it off to the lab where they had a six-month backlog of cases. It was unhelpful in burglary cases where the detectives liked to close out a case in a few days or a few weeks. Fingerprints were the workhorses of evidence collection. In just a few minutes, they could be entered into a computer on site or at the crime lab by our fabulous print technician Mandy, and the computer would spit out the results. Unlike the nifty machines on the TV shows, our computer display didn't show the fingerprint on the screen. It didn't link up the points and show where the print matched. All it did was show the names of ten individuals in the sort of green lettering found on mid-1980s computers. Then Mandy could print out the scanned-in fingerprint cards of the top matches and compare them herself to ensure that the prints matched.

Fingerprinting is an art more than a science. There are different powders and brushes depending on the surface and powder type. If you use a camel-hair brush on a print that's too fragile, the brush bristles will magically wipe the print away. If you use an ostrich-feather brush on powder that's too coarse, you'll damage the feathers of the brush and it won't help you develop good prints. If you've sprayed ninhydrin on a paper and you're holding a steam iron over it to develop the prints (because ninhydrin reacts with the amino acids left by the oils in your hands and turns them pink when hit with moist heat) but you hold the iron too close, you'll overdevelop the prints and the detail will be lost. In graduate school, we had an entire semester devoted to development and preservation of fingerprints. Of course, the best way to preserve fingerprints is to superglue-fume the object, because the superglue sticks to the prints and creates a hard coating so that they won't rub off (the downside to this is that if you fume it for too long, the glue will fill in the details between the ridges and thus make your print unusable). Then again, most of this is moot, because the chances of finding a useable, unsmudged fingerprint at a crime scene are infuriatingly low, yet tantalizingly possible. They are the bane and joy of any CSI.

The burglaries and robberies had been going on for weeks. Convenience stores everywhere in the city were on high alert and the lab personnel spent most of our time running from QuikTrip (the 7-Eleven of Wichita) to Walgreens and then on over to Kum-n-go (I swear I am not making that name up). This guy was good. He always wore a mask and gloves and was never in a place for longer than forty-five seconds. He would wave a gun in someone's face, demand the money in the cash register, and run out. When we looked at the surveillance tapes, we saw that he was usually hunched over, and seemed to wear a lot of clothing, but we really couldn't tell. The footage was grainy and the tapes had been used over and over again, until they were nearly useless. Most convenience stores at the time used a system that just started the same tape over again when it ran out of space. It saved time and money, and really, who needed more than the past six hours of footage anyway? After all, robberies are called in almost the minute they happen and burglaries of such stores are usually discovered within an hour of the time the crime was committed. But taping over and over on the same tape caused the quality of the recording material to burn out quickly, and thus we were left with a general grayish shape on the video, which might have been a person waving a gun and wearing a lot of clothing, or possibly a small elephant waving its trunk around in a desperate search for a bucket of water. It was, to say the least, not helpful. But one thing we did know. The suspect always wore gloves. The clerks all confirmed it and in some of the better quality surveillance videos we could see that was true. And more often than not, he never even touched anything in the store, because the doors were automatic. He even brought his own plastic bags with him for the money, so he never even had to reach for anything. He just shoved the cash in the bag and left. We had nothing. No evidence. No real scene, just some photographs of the building, a measurement of the door, which was really useless, and a surveillance tape that no one could possibly use to identify anyone. The big map on the wall in the lab was a kaleidoscope of colored dots as the detectives looked for any sort of pattern to the robberies. Did he hit Walgreens more often or QuikTrips? Did he focus on one area of town more than another? Was he working his way from east to west across the city? Did he only go to Kum-n-Go on Tuesdays in the early afternoon hours? They were grasping at straws because there was no pattern that we could see. He would hit one place, drive a mile down the road and hit another one. But the problem was, in the city, a mile is a long distance, and in between the two stores that got robbed were sixteen other convenience stores that had apparently escaped his notice. It had been three weeks and counting since the whole thing started, over one hundred stores had been robbed, and we were all absolutely stymied. Even the informants of the narcotics detectives were coming up with a big fat zero. Public service announcements and reward numbers started airing on local newscasts. All the patrol officers were on hyper-alert for anyone wearing gloves and a mask. Of course, this was the middle of winter in Wichita and nearly everyone was wearing gloves and a ski mask because the wind chill was minus ten degrees and no one wanted to get frostbite just to prove to passing patrols that they weren't convenience store robbers. Even the voice over the police radio seemed to be tired of reporting the same thing over and over again. "Lab needed at 2490 Bremers Road for a robbery." I could hear the apathy in her voice. We were all getting demoralized. Only Patti, Pat, and I were on duty that day, and as Patti and Pat were already on other robberies, I swung the van around and headed back to Bremers Road. I switched my radio to a private channel and asked the officer at the scene.

"Hey, QuikTrip or Walgreens?" I asked.

"QuikTrip," came back the reply, and I could hear the sigh in Dave's voice.

"Dave?" I checked just to be sure.

"Hey, LabLaura."

"Anything new on this one?"

"Not so far." I could feel the frustration as he clicked off the radio.

Dave had tried out several nicknames for me over the course of my time at the lab. "Scully" seemed appropriate since I was a forensic person and had the red hair, but it never stuck. When he found out I had wanted to be an archaeologist when I was a child, he tried "Indy," but that just never seemed right. However, "LabLaura" worked fairly well and was one that even I, with my sensitivity to nicknames ever since my band director, who I hit with the side with my flute, called me "Little Merz" in the 7th grade to distinguish me from my older sister couldn't object to. No one else bothered to call me that name, but then again, it didn't matter. I only had two close friends on the police force, Heather and Dave, and of course in the lab, I adored Patti. I think the best way to sum it up was that I had brought each one to the Vagabond, and they had then begun going there on their own, and that, of course, made them family. So if the rest of the officers didn't know my nickname, or my real name for that matter, it was all right with me. I loved working scenes with Dave because we always had things to talk about besides the case at hand. Sometimes, when you're spreading fingerprint powder around or snapping a hundred photographs, the best thing to think about is something else entirely, and Dave had a never-ending supply of topics. His latest concern was about a personal electromagnetic field that he seemed to have. Wherever he went, computers crashed, cell phones broke, and electric appliances seemed to give up the ghost. He had even been able to crash an Apple computer—something that the store representatives just couldn't understand. They kept trying to insist that their computers did not give one the blue screen of death, but somehow, Dave's computer managed to do it—and all he had done was walk into the room.

When I arrived at the QuikTrip, I was greeted by a single police vehicle with flashing lights. This just proved how commonplace these robberies had become. In times past, an armed robbery was good for at least three police vehicles and possibly several onlookers. In times past, an armed robbery was the biggest thing going on around this town. But now, a lone police vehicle with two officers was enough to handle it. I took my photographs and waved to Dave, who was interviewing the clerk. The clerk looked a little shaken, but not really traumatized by the events of the night. He had heard about the robberies, and come tomorrow morning, he'd be boasting to his friends that he had been held up by the Wichita Bandit, as well. He might even invent a moment of bravery, where he brandished a baseball bat at the bandit before the bandit threatened him with a gun. I could see the story forming in his head.

Dave looked at me. "Shall we check the video?" I nodded. Sure. Why not? I was able to watch M*A*S*H reruns over and over again with my dad, so watching a few minutes of a video that I had seen so many times shouldn't be a problem. The grainy picture jumped around on the screen. Man, this videotape was in bad shape. The robber walked through the automatic doors, pulled out his gun, and yelled something at the clerk. He pulled the bag out from his pocket and jerked his arm up and down to open it. The clerk put the money in the bag... "Wait. Dave, go back a few frames." I looked again. When he pulled the bag out of his pocket, something fell to the floor. I couldn't see what it was, and it was out of the frame of the surveillance camera. But something definitely came out of his pocket. After he got the money, he ran out through the automatic doors, but he didn't bend over or pick anything up. Whatever it was might still be around. We went back out to the main area of the store. I stood in front of the counter. And then bent down to look under the overhang near the floor. There, just under the overhang, was a plastic bag. A wadded-up plastic Walmart bag. Crap. The only thing he had dropped was the bag for his next heist. And he had been wearing gloves when it had fallen out of his pocket. I photographed the bag and collected it. At least now we knew that he shopped at Walmart. Or worked there. Or that someone in his household shopped at Walmart. Or worked there. I mentioned that to Dave and he laughed. "Well, girl, that narrows it down to everyone in this city but the two of us."

We had been trying to avoid Walmart as the evil corporation that took away the customers of small businesses. Problem was that as the small businesses closed down, there weren't that many other places left to get certain items. "Dave, I should tell you, there was this one time when I needed batteries for my remote control..." Dave hushed me. "Well, anyone can fall off the wagon once. Just last week I really needed a small stepladder and the hardware store by my house was closed for the evening..."

Okay, we didn't know anything more than before, but at least I had one more piece of evidence than anyone else had found from this knucklehead.

"Hey, I finished the book you loaned me." Dave was the only police officer to ever borrow books from my personal library. It was one of the reasons I adored him. He was also the only openly gay officer on the police force, which often put him in positions of ridicule and disrespect among the other officers. Never mind that he was stronger, smarter, and braver than most of them. They would never say anything outright discriminatory to his face, but it always lurked there just below the surface. One day, we knew, he'd be promoted to detective. One day, we knew, he'd be recognized as the great officer that he was. He just had to wait out the old guard in the top management spots. Either that or sue for discrimination, but that seemed like it would cause far more problems than he wanted to deal with. "You mind if I loan it out to someone else?" "No, I don't mind. I'm all for the sharing of ideas." I smiled and drove off back to the lab.

Plastic bags are lousy for fingerprints. You can't use powder or ninhydrin on them. And I had no idea if superglue-fuming would work, even if there were fingerprints on the bag. It was crumpled and had been smushed in a jacket pocket. But it was worth a shot and Mandy said that she wasn't going to need the fuming chamber for the rest of the day. I opened up the bag and clipped the handles to the bar at the top of the chamber. It was suspended above the floor so that the fumes could get to all the sides and bottom of the bag, as well as the inside area. Mandy thought that twenty-five minutes would be about the right time. We wouldn't be able to see anything after it was all done, but with some dye stain and an alternate light source, well, the best we could do was take a look. I felt like I was back in school in the little lab room with all the crime scene supplies doing a research project on superglue-fuming and plastic bags. I used rhodamine, a fluorescent dye stain that works really well under an alternate light source (ALS), to light up any areas where there was superglue (which should be just around fingerprints or smudges of fingerprints). But it's super hard to photograph: it can take eleven or twelve tries to get the lighting right, and not only that, but the film for the very specialized camera we used for those sorts of things was $2.00 a frame. The lab director would make grumbling noises about budgets and waste every time he walked by and watched us toss one of the pictures out in frustration because the lighting didn't work and the entire thing came out too dark to be useful for comparison. The film was a special type of Polaroid film, so you had your picture develop in a matter of seconds. But that meant you couldn't see if you had the lighting right until after it was developed, and therein lay the problem. I squeezed out the dye on the now fumed bag, and attempted to make sure I hit every part, because it would be just my luck that there would be a print on the bag, but I would miss it because the dye stain hadn't gotten to that area. I turned on the ALS to a wavelength of 535 nanometers and put on my colored goggles. There were the occasional areas of fluorescence where the chemical had seeped into a crease on the bag, but other than that, nothing. I turned it inside out and began again. About midway into my examination of the other side, I saw ridge detail. I saw lots of ridge detail. I saw a whorl pattern with two deltas. The very best parts of a fingerprint for identification. I stared. This just wasn't possible. This just didn't happen. Well, it did happen, but only on TV and even then, only to the best examiners. I glanced about surreptitiously for a television crew, possibly from Candid Camera, but none were forthcoming.

"Hey, Mandy! Mandy, come see!" I was as excited as any child who has just built her first block tower. Mandy came running over. "It's good enough, right?" I asked just to be sure. Mandy bent down low. "Oh Laura, it's gorgeous! Let's get it photographed and entered!" We both fussed over that Walmart bag with its one fingerprint as if it were the crown jewels of England. We fluttered, we babbled, and in the end, after only seven tries, we got a picture worthy to enter into AFIS (the Automated Fingerprint Identification System). Now we had to hope that this person had been arrested before and thus his prints would be in the system. I crossed my fingers. Come on … miracle! Come on, Candid Camera crew and all the CSI gods. Come on. Let this work out. We deserve this. We've been to too many scenes where there's been nothing to work with. We need this.

"You do realize that it'll take a couple of hours to run, right?" Mandy said in amusement, "You can open your eyes and uncross your fingers for a while."

I opened my eyes, nodded and went to my computer to start typing the report. Come on, I thought. Let this work. If this works I promise I'll never disparage CSI again. No wait, that's far too unrealistic. If this works I promise I will never throw my slippers at the TV set when the investigators go into a crime scene and don't turn on the lights. Yes, okay. I can live with that one. I can not throw things. I go entire days without throwing things so that's one promise I can keep.

"Hey Laura, we've got results!" Mandy called out.

At this point I should say a word about AFIS results. Normally, AFIS gives the top ten matches on the screen in the form of FBI numbers or names of the people who have been entered into the system. If the fingerprint matches any of them, 99 times out of 100 it will be the first person on the list. The computer will say that it matches at a very high percentage rate to that person's prints, and options two through ten will be very low percentages of matches. If the print hasn't been scanned into the system, all ten matches can be low percentages. However, computers can make mistakes, prints can be blurry, or the scan of the fingerprint card could be bad. That's why a human being has to go in and check to make sure that the prints actually do match.

Mandy was pulling up the first result before I could see if it had a high percentage match. I waited. And waited. And waited. Mandy is an excellent, very thorough fingerprint examiner, which is great when you have her in the witness box on the stand and she can go through point by point and explain to a jury what she looked at, and what she compared, but it's infuriating when you're hovering over her shoulder waiting for a result. After all, she didn't know which finger this was, so she had to compare it to all ten fingerprints on the card of the first person on the list. Please, please, let this be my CSI moment, I pleaded. Please Grissom and Booth, and the girl whose name I can't remember but she played the wife that got killed in the movie Memento with the really hot guy whose name I can't remember right now either. Please! I hovered. She moved her hand with the jewelers' loupe down to the second row of prints, and stopped. There it was. I knew it from the way her shoulders tensed. She had it. We had our suspect. This is him! She gave me the biggest grin and ran over to tell the detective in charge of the burglary department. I slumped back into my chair. "Thank god," I thought, "that I didn't promise not to disparage CSI anymore." It was going to be hard enough to refrain from throwing my slippers.

CHAPTER SEVENTEEN
Anatomy Of a Crime Scene

Four bullets, two men, one woman. One car, one bike, one gun. When you break it down the pieces seem so small, but they add up to one incontrovertible fact—one man is dead. And somehow the people who loved him need answers. They need me to tell them why and how and did he suffer—and the truth is, I can't. Grissom I am not—would that I were like him. Able to both comfort and keep my dispassionate distance. I didn't know this victim, but I kept choking up, tears at the ready behind glasses that I was glad were reflecting the flashing lights rather than allowing access to my eyes.

The bullets tore his head apart and broke his girlfriend's heart at the same time. I didn't want to keep talking to her. She stood hovering at the tape, leaning over on tiptoe, willing herself beyond the barrier, lifting, straining for that extra inch nearer to the man she had made love to an hour before. I knew this because she told me in Spanish that I thought I had forgotten as I tried to get the facts of his life from her. All I needed were his name, birth date, address, phone number— the numbers that create a paper life at the top of a resume. I did not want to know that he kissed her before he left, or that he never swore when she was around. I didn't want to know that he dreamed of owning one truly great classic car, fully restored. She poured out the words to me in a torrent that I could not dam up. She needed to tell someone and I was easy prey, notebook in hand, able to interject only a small "Cuándo nació?" into the conversation, which I hoped meant, "When was he born?" Her hands fluttered as she spoke, clutching the air, and then releasing it. Had she been catching fireflies she would have held them too tightly, releasing them only to have their bodies fall through the night to the pavement. Would that have been a fitting tribute to him? Here, darling, let me surround you with those that also no longer shine in the night. Why did she single me out? Could she hear the laughter in the male voices around us? Perhaps a double

X chromosome was enough to convince her of a connection.

He's a gang member, I kept telling myself. Once an eight-year-old boy had died because of him. Six years ago he had been destined to die, the gun had been aimed at him, only to find a smaller target on his first bike without training wheels. Somehow fitting, then, now that his bike lay in the road, useless. I wanted to tell her that I didn't care. That I was sorry for her loss, but I wanted to get behind my camera lens to filter out the emotion. Let the cross hairs of the lens follow the path of the bullets. I wanted that isolation I so desperately despise at three in the morning. I wanted him to be alive. I wanted him to get up, take off the fake arrow headband, and laugh at the ruckus he started. I wanted the words "April fools" and "I got you" to spring from his mouth that lay slightly askew on his face right then. I made my escape with barely a "lo siento" for his friends. Grabbed my camera, looked at the flashing lights through the viewfinder. I often wonder if it can help me choose my own view. I'd have liked to be looking at the ocean right then, the ocean in daylight with a sun so bright the sand seems to burn the air. I wanted a point of view different than the one I had. Different than the officers around me. An alternative reality viewed only through my camera.

Seventeen photographs. There was really not much of a scene there. A body, a bike, some blood. That was all that I had to work with. It wouldn't take long. Measure the road, take a swab of blood, collect the bike. It was so routine, too easy. There was no bullet. There were no exit wounds. The lead that took him away was still inside of him. The crowd didn't understand that I didn't have a TV crew to give me filler for the next hour. Efficiency works for public relations in so many jobs; why must mine be in the minority? How do I explain I have more questions than answers for the bereaved? When questions are the enemy, am I spying on the other side or joining it? I wished I could take his necklace and press it into her hand. I wished I could replace this view with a happy memory for her. Instead, I helped him into the bag, zipped up the cover to hide the holes in his face with blue plastic and nylon. Took off my gloves inside out to avoid his blood contaminating me. Drove away from the red and blue strobe effect in the night.

I forgot to get his phone number for my report. If I looked it up and called, would someone answer?

CHAPTER EIGTEEN
The Dating Game

I don't answer my personal cell phone when I'm at crime scenes. First of all, I often don't have it with me at a scene, as I prefer to leave it in the van (since my pockets are generally full of things like flashlights, powders, brushes, chemical test kits, my sketch book, and some writing implements). But also, I don't answer it because my gloves are often dirty with body fluids or black powder, and really, who wants that on her cell phone? It's bad enough that the screens get gunk on them from the oils on our faces, but who wants other contaminants on her phone?

Most of my friends knew that I didn't answer my phone during my shift and would always wait until after 11 p.m. to call me, when they figured I'd be off work. So I was a little surprised to see a message waiting for me when I got back in the van after a burglary scene, especially since I didn't recognize the telephone number.

"Hey, Laura, this is James Moretti. Listen, I finished reading your book, the one that Dave loaned me, and I'd like to discuss it with you. Do you want to get dinner tomorrow night?"

I stared at my phone. Had I just been asked out via voicemail? Or was this really a book discussion question? I called up an image of James Moretti, albeit a somewhat hazy one. He had gone out with Dave and me one time, or rather, I had gone out with them once.

We had gone to one of the few gay clubs in Wichita, since Dave wanted to dance, and neither James nor I cared where we went, so long as the people were fun to talk to. I like gay clubs because usually the men are better looking, know how to dance, and never even try to grope a passing girl. And I had thought James was cute at the time, cute enough for me to steal his baseball cap while we were on the dance floor, but that was several months ago now. Plus, he had mentioned that he had kids later on that night, and I had assumed he was married and just out on the town one night with

Dave. I put him out of my mind after that, because I don't ever date or flirt with guys who are already taken.

So why on earth had he called me now? I was free for dinner the following night; after all, tomorrow was Wednesday and the first day of my weekend. But was he married? And did he have kids? This needed some quick research. I called Dave. "Hey, Dave, want to go get something at Denny's after work?"

"Sure," came back the response. We had both had busy shifts and hadn't had time to eat. At Denny's I attempted to think of a casual way to bring up the voicemail from James, but couldn't. I'm not very good with pretext conversations.

"So, James Moretti called me and said that he wanted to take me to dinner to discuss my book that you loaned him. Isn't he married?" Dave looked surprised.

"He's divorced. One of those Kansas high school marriages that didn't work out and only lasted a couple of years," Dave replied.

I nodded.

"What do you think?" I asked. I knew Dave and James were good friends and Dave would give me an honest assessment.

"Oh, you should go out with him!" Dave gushed. "I've been in locker rooms with him, and Laura, he's hung like a horse!"

This was not, perhaps, the first thing I looked for in a man when I started to date someone, but the enthusiastic tone made me pause. I looked at Dave.

"But he's nice too, right?"

Dave smiled.

"He's the most romantic person I've met and you know I wouldn't be friends with someone who wasn't a quality person, Laura. Sure, go out with him."

And with that endorsement I called James back. And woke him up. Because although it was early in the evening for me, I worked second shift and thus was routinely awake until 2 a.m. when the Vagabond closed. James, on the other hand, was a general contractor and had to wake up at five in the morning. But even though he seemed somewhat befuddled on the phone, we agreed that he would pick me up at my apartment around 5:30 the following day.

Oh, lord, I thought to myself. A date? What did one do on dates these days? What would I wear? I loved being a CSI because I never had to decide what to wear. I wore a uniform, for crying out loud. It was the best thing—I'd look in my closet and think, "Gee, should I wear the blue uniform, or the blue uniform? Ah well, it doesn't matter."

And I had been out with guys before in Wichita, but they were all guys from the Vagabond, and we were all friends there. They had seen me at my worst, when I stumbled in at 1:45 just past last call, so tired from overtime at crime scenes, but needing a chai tea like nothing else in the world. (I often wondered if the bartenders put heroin in my tea, since I couldn't remember having an addiction to chai when I lived in New York.) They had seen me at my best. They knew my stories and my history. They knew my clothing was perpetually covered in cat fur because Pyewacket, aside from being the best companion I could have asked for, also turned out to be the kind of cat that lost his body weight in hair on an hourly basis.

James was an unknown entity. I was about to call in reinforcements and get my hair done when, luckily, common sense took hold. I was finding this happened more and more as I worked crime scenes. Something about seeing people on the worst day of their lives, and watching everyone squirm as they told lies about their actions at a scene, made me just want to be myself without pretenses when I was out with people. At a scene, it was my job to strip away the pretenses and the distractions to find out the truth. Concealing the truth about myself to other people had become ludicrous. James would just have to deal with who I really was.

He picked me up at 5:30 on the dot. I didn't mention it, but this was my first time in a pickup truck. I usually railed against people who drove trucks and SUVs around the city and never even made it off the paved roads, since clearly they were just buying big cars and contributing to global warming because they thought a big car was a better status symbol.

Once, my neighbor bought himself a Hummer, though I knew he only used it to drive to the grocery store and work, both of which were only a mile and a half away. As he looked at his new toy with pride he asked me, "So, what do you think?" and without pausing to consult my inner filter, I blurted out, "I think you have a really tiny penis and are compensating." Which, while truly what I thought, did not make it any less embarrassing for either of us. But he did return it that day and came back with a Prius, which says a lot more about his manhood than anything else he could have done.

But James was a contractor who built houses and used his truck to haul wood, supplies, and other such things for work, so I refrained from mentioning my natural assumption that large vehicles generally mean small genitalia. Besides, Dave wouldn't lie to me.

We laughed through dinner. I told James stories of crime scenes and how I once rescued an iguana on my college campus in New York City, and he told me stories of his time as a medic in the Army and the work he did in South America. We spoke about personal histories and family, and of future vacations that we both needed but never took the time off of work to enjoy. He had taken me to a Greek restaurant, which was both daring of a Wichita guy and spoke well of his food choices. I could feel myself falling for him, and tried desperately to stop myself. I didn't fall for someone in one date. I was too sensible for that! I needed further evidence and to weigh the pros and cons of dating someone before I decided if I liked him. I lost the battle as we got into the truck after dinner.

"Do you want to go see a movie or to a club?" I asked him.

"To be honest, I'd rather talk with you some more. You want to show me the Vagabond?" he responded. And then and there, I fell in love with James Moretti.

"Why did you call me yesterday?" I asked James as we sat at the back table of the Vagabond. James smiled just a little cockily.

"Well, Dave told me how you had asked him for my phone number and how he hadn't given it to you since he didn't have my permission, and I just thought that was crazy. So I got your number from him and gave you a call."

I nodded.

His posture was definitely taking on a little bit of a macho persona and I did so enjoy bursting those sorts of moments.

"Yeah. That ... never happened. Seems like our buddy Dave set us up. Didn't you find it odd that in his story, he wouldn't give me your number without permission, but he very readily gave you mine?"

James stopped and then burst out laughing. "Never occurred to me! I guess that's why you're the investigator." We smiled as we held eye contact. "Guess it doesn't matter now."

We talked at the Vagabond until 1:30 in the morning, when I finally noticed James was barely keeping his eyes open. He had been up since five at work, and would have to get up in another three-and-a-half hours for a full workday again.

"I think we're both a little tired. Why don't we call it a night? I know you have to get up soon." James nodded.

"I don't want to, but you're right."

We paid and left. Pete leaned over to me as I left a $10 tip for our $6 of drinks.

"Hang on to him," he told me. I looked at him quizzically. Pete hadn't been at our table much, and there was no possible way he could know how I was feeling. He winked at me.

"You always entertain us," he pointed out. "But no one has made you laugh like that in all the time you've been here."

I smiled at him as I walked out the door. For the first time, I didn't feel the pang of my crush on Pete as I left the bar.

As we pulled up to my apartment building, I turned to James. This was the part I always hated about dates. The awkward car moment. That moment when you don't know if you should lean in for a kiss or just sit there, or get out of the car. I loathed that moment because both people were nervous and trying to figure out how the other person felt. People, in my opinion, should be honest with each other and with themselves. I wanted that goodnight kiss. I was pretty sure James did, too. So why put us both through a few minutes of awkwardness? As I unbuckled my seatbelt, I smiled at James.

"I hate the awkward car moment," I told him. "So if you want a kiss goodnight, you'll just have to get out of the car."

I've never seen a man move so quickly in my life. By the time my seatbelt was unbuckled and resting in its holder, James had gotten out of his seatbelt, opened his door, leapt out of the car, run around the front of the truck, and opened my door for me.

Victory is mine, I crowed in my head. But as we leaned in, and I closed my eyes, the thought came unbidden, Victory is Ours.

I drove to the hospital to pick up the victim's clothing and the rape kit, as well as the suspect's clothing and rape kit. And I heard the nurses whispering.

"She's out now, poor thing."

"We're putting her on suicide watch—she asked us to kill her because she doesn't want to live anymore."

I heard snippets about the injuries. Her lip was split. Her eye was swollen shut. She had a broken wrist. She was bleeding from the anus. And the vagina. There was a bite mark on her shoulder that was bleeding as well. Her clothing was torn. Three fingernails were broken. The suspect had scratches on his face around his eyes. They thought she tried to gouge his eyes out with her nails.

The detectives looked at each other. He was saying it was consensual and that she liked it rough. He said it took him a while to ejaculate and that it was her first anal sex experience and maybe he went a little too fast. He said he did nothing wrong and she never objected to anything he did.

The clothing I collected from him includes a US Air Force t-shirt, among other things. There was more blood on that.

CHAPTER NINETEEN
The Beleaguered Bank Robber

When you are robbing a bank, don't attempt to do it from the drive-through window.

You see, the drive-through window is bulletproof plastic, and the bank tellers don't feel particularly threatened when they have that between you and them, plus a wall, plus those neat little tubes that suck up your banking requests to the secret portal in the money bin. In fact, they most likely feel a remarkable sense of calm, mingled with amusement and disbelief that someone would try to rob a bank through the drive-through.

But some people are not deterred by thoughts of failure or ridicule. Some people don't worry about what others think. I'm not one of those people. I'd be concerned that I would be (a) laughed at and (b) arrested and sent to prison for attempted bank robbery, but this man was not afraid of such things. This man decided to rob a bank from the convenience of his air-conditioned vehicle. Not just any bank, mind you. His own bank. The bank he's banked with for years. The one where, like Norm in Cheers, and me at the Vagabond, everyone knows his name—in part because his uniform, which he generally wore into the bank when he made his deposits and withdrawals, has his name right on it.

Maybe it was me, but somehow the crimes in Wichita seemed to be getting easier to solve. One recent day I'd had a drive-by shooting that involved an assailant on a bicycle who attempted to look cool, rather than aim his gun, so he held it out sideways like the gangsters do on TV. I'm sure he did look very cool for the split second between when he pulled the trigger and when the recoil knocked him off his bike and he sprawled on the ground and was held there by various irate residents who didn't want guns fired at their houses. Not that he hit anything mind you. You can't hit something when you hold the gun sideways and don't aim.

Whenever I was called out to a shooting scene, I made it a point to ask the age of the shooter, if known, and if he was under the age of twenty, I'd get out my metal detector and check the ground about six feet in front of where he had stood. Because chances were, the bullets were in the ground since he tried to look cool by holding the gun sideways. The gangsters of Wichita: style, yes; substance, no. Hitting the broad side of a barn would have been an improvement for most of them.

But back to this gem of Wichita, who drove up to the bank, put a note in the little portal, and watched it get sucked up to the magic place where the bank teller sits. She waved to him. He waved back. She read the note. It said, "This is a robbery. Give me all your money."

That was it. No quantification of what "all your money" meant. It could have meant all the money she had on her at the time, which probably would have amounted to about $30 in her wallet. Or had he meant the sum total of the money that the bank held in cash on hand, in bonds, and electronically? There was no real way to judge.

The teller hit the panic button, and then, thinking quickly, wrote a note back saying, "Hold on a second, Larry! I'm getting the money ready for you!" She knew his name, account number, and address because he'd been banking there for years. And she also knew that Larry did have some money in his bank account, so if she gave him some and he somehow got away with the crime, the bank would just take it as a withdrawal from his own account.

So Larry, trusting his friendly neighborhood bank teller, sat in his car. And waited.

And then the FBI showed up and arrested a very bewildered Larry. When I arrived, he was saying, "But Sharlene said she was getting me the money," in a very plaintive manner.

I suppose he felt betrayed. After all, he had been banking there for years and had an account in good standing. It was bad manners for the teller to inform him she was getting the money together and then to call the police.

I suppose I can see certain advantages to robbing a bank where you have an account. After all, you can rob the place and then make a deposit, thus eliminating all evidence as the money goes from the bank to the bank, just in a different account.

But still, I'm thinking they might catch on to that scheme.

CHAPTER TWENTY
Ladykillers

A girl I knew killed herself one day. I investigated the scene. I didn't really know her. But I'd smiled at her before. She worked in a movie theater I'd been to. I saw Big Fish there. She told me which screen it was playing on. I smiled and brushed by her with a quick "thanks." She smiled back, but even then, she didn't smile with her eyes. I assumed that it was because she was working in a movie theater and fake-smiled at hundreds of movie patrons each day. And then I let myself be transported to another world by Tim Burton. I didn't once look at her nametag. I didn't call her by her name, and I hadn't once thought about her since that time. I didn't even really think about her then. I was too excited to see a movie with some friends.

I don't remember her being pretty, but I do remember how she looked when she was alive. Her hair was brown with highlights that weren't done by a stylist. She had freckles.

This day, her face was mottled purple. She had been lying on her stomach when she died and the blood settled. By the time she was found, lividity was fixed in the skin. No embalmer can fix that. Her nose was pushed in somewhat and a yellow-orange fluid came from her nose as her body purged.

She had worn her bra to bed. The methadone bottle was empty and lay where she had dropped it. The scattered Lortabs quickly showed that there were far too few of them to make up what should have remained in the prescription bottle. I wondered what had happened to her. Was she depressed? She was certainly addicted to painkillers, we had a police history on that in the computer system under her name. Did she have a lot of friends? Why wasn't there a grieving mother asking to say goodbye to her? Had something so awful happened in her childhood that the weight of it finally crushed her under it? Did she know when she painted her toenails that this would be the last color they would ever see?

She was twenty-five. So was I.

I left. There was a case waiting. EMCU had called—that stands for Emergency Medical Children's Unit. I hate EMCU calls. They're never good. They usually let me see just how low humans can sink. This time, they had removed a five-year-old girl from her home. Her father had been sexually abusing her for the past year. The signed search warrant awaited me.

Rape scenes are difficult for me as it is. Child rape scenes are the stuff of nightmares. Have you ever watched a TV show where the toys are evil? Or clowns are the scariest thing anyone can imagine? The dolls stare down at you with an unholy aspect? The TV producers have it all wrong. The scariest thing anyone can do with toys is examine them for trace evidence and body fluids.

Try getting out a UV light as dispassionately as possible and running it over Eeyore's countenance to see if ejaculation occurred there. Try doing tape lifts of a teddy bear. Then take that toy, put a tag around its paw (a toe tag, declaring it to be no longer a plaything, but dead to the innocent world of Neverland) and place it in a plain brown paper bag. Seal the bag. Make a note—brown pubic hairs on the face of the Raggedy Ann doll (my victim is blonde). Run a UV light over sheets that proudly display the PowerPuff girls, the cartoon characters that exclaim Girl Power and show six-year-olds with enormous eyes beating up evil monkeys.

I've seen worse. I've seen younger victims. I've seen rooms with more body fluids. But the porn gets to me. This is a child's room. The tables are low, the chairs are too small for most adults to sink into. There are videotapes out that don't belong here. They show naked women and are named Double D Vixens and Hello Kiddie. The unlabeled tapes terrify me. I keep hoping they're not homemade. They all glow in the light of my ALS. They've been masturbated on and never cleaned. They're sitting on the same shelf as the Strawberry Shortcake tapes. Those tapes glow too. I don't know which is worse. Yes, I do. I don't want Strawberry Shortcake tapes to fluoresce.

One of the teddy bears glows faintly, but all over. Especially where its right arm meets its torso. It doesn't look like the right kind of glow for semen. I know this. I know what semen looks like in this light. I know what it looks like when the light is purple and I wear my orange goggles. This isn't quite right. I wonder if it's urine, but that doesn't quite match up either.

It isn't until I look at the pads on its paws that I see it. Particulate matter. Granules within the glow. This bear isn't used by the father. This is a Comfort Bear. Salt tears are giving it a halo.

I wonder if in twenty years someone will be looking at this girl, as she lies dead of a drug overdose, wondering if something happened in her past that finally crushed her under its weight.

CHAPTER TWENTY-ONE

The Great Gatorade Caper

When called out to a crime scene, there are usually a few possibilities of what I'm going to find when I get there. There can be hysterical or excited people, tears, confusion, flashing lights, or a calm person who can relay the details quickly and in order. Sometimes, unfortunately, it's much more difficult to work a crime scene. The victim tends to get in the way and will not allow us to do our jobs. He follows us around and gives advice or attempts to help and then ends up contaminating the scene and ruining our evidence. And he does this because he has seen CSI, or worse yet, CSI Miami. Oh, it's a bad day when the victim has seen these shows. Because then they believe that they can solve crimes themselves, or point me in the right direction. Such cases are at the very pinnacle of frustration for the police and laboratory personnel.

I had an armed robbery at a convenience store one night. The clerk, an excitable young man of seventeen, was thrilled at the idea of being robbed. He had seen the shows! He knew the information I needed! He could state with certainty that the suspect had stolen not only money, but also a bottle of Gatorade! As he made this pronouncement, he looked up in surprise, as if shocked by the lack of ominous music emanating from the walls. I explained that generally in real life, crime scenes do not come with their own soundtracks other than police sirens. And he was not content to let his memory serve him as we asked him what the suspect touched. He ran to the back room and beckoned us to follow to watch the tape. Because that way he could point excitedly at the tape during the critical time periods and say, "That's it! That's him!" It was a good thing he did that, because as a trained investigator I would not have realized the man waving the gun was a robber. I would have figured him for the average, skulking, gun-waving convenience store patron. I nodded gravely.

"I see. Thank you, sir." The officer behind me let out a cough that sounded remarkably un-coughlike. Kind of a cross between a sneeze and a snort that did a flip halfway through the dismount and landed as a wheeze. And then IT happened. Our young man froze the tape and in a frenzy of Grissom worship announced, "He stole an ORANGE Gatorade!" The triumph in his eye was unmistakable. He knew he had just solved the case for us. This was the break we had all been waiting for and he had provided it! We needed to put out an APB for all orange-Gatorade-drinking folk! Surely, there couldn't be more than one of them in the state of Kansas! It takes a lot of control to nod sagely at such times. Luckily, I have years of theater training from high school and college and the character that always works in such situations is Aunt Eller from Oklahoma. She's a hardy old woman who doesn't take nonsense from anyone, but makes sure that those who mean well are recognized for their efforts. I summoned up my best impression of her and nodded. "Good work, young man. Good work."

In the TV shows, the crime scene investigators pick up a hair, or a blade of grass, or a bit of a toenail, and have a flashback to the crime scene. They see the suspect kick in the door, and break his toenail. They see him take off his shoe and dump the piece of toenail out. They see him then go off and kill the victim or steal the gold, or whatever it is he intended to do. I have never had this happen to me. I have never picked up a blade of grass from the floor and suddenly seen the suspect romping through a field of flowers with his dog, and the dog gets shot, thus inducing the suspect's homicidal rage. I've never known his thought process as he commits a crime, but as the young man seemed so intent on making the armed robbery into a TV episode, I decided to attempt to understand the psyche of this master criminal. As I pictured it, his thought process might go like this: "Hmm ... I'm really thirsty, think I'll go to the gas station and get some Gatorade. Mmm ... Gatorade. What flavor should I get? Red, orange, or blue, so many choices. Think I'll go with orange. Yeah. Orange Gatorade. It's like orange juice but without the pulp. But I bet lots of football players drink it. Yeah, they show that on TV all the time. Whoops, forgot I don't have any cash on me. Damn. No orange Gatorade for me! But I really want it! Hey, maybe I'll use this gun! Then I can get some money and the Gatorade! Damn, I'm smart. I am so smart. Smart! Heh. They'll never catch me."

Somehow, this seemed more likely than the criminal thoughts of the people on TV, but probably did not make for the high drama demanded by the viewing public.

I tried to think of ways to increase the drama of the situation. Was it significant that orange is the color code the police use to identify people who are mentally unstable? Maybe this person was attempting to communicate the idea that he's insane. Maybe he robbed a lot of gas stations and took one bottle of orange Gatorade each time. And what if there was no orange Gatorade? Would he take a different color, or would he be stuck, unsure of whether to rob the place or move on to the next gas station, which would surely be better stocked with beverages? Would he consider other sports drinks, or would he be forced into choosing soda instead?

The mind just boggled. Perhaps we needed to call in Grissom. He'd probably be able to enhance the tape to see the fibers on the guy's t-shirt, made of Alpaca wool. Such wool is sold in only one store in town. Such a shirt has only been purchased by one man. That man has an addiction to orange Gatorade! And better yet, all those details are in a database that the police can easily access from their computers. Need a database of sneaker impressions? Sure! They've got that on TV. How about a database of carpet fibers? Yep, luckily Gil Grissom has that too.

It's always a complicated, complex, highly improbable solution. The DNA would show that the robber is the long-lost half brother of the gas station attendant, who was kidnapped when he was two years old and had grown up without the love and support of his family. He blames this on his brother, and decided to rob the place to get even.

My problem is, I'm just not a dramatic enough person. I don't have that Hollywood flair. I'm content to dust the glass of the door where the suspect placed his ungloved hand firmly to open the door and leave. I'm content with lifting those fingerprints and running them through the lab computer where Mandy is able to match them to a suspect.

This is not a good television show. There's no suspense. There's no twist in the case. But I will be sure to list the total loss of the store as fifty bucks and one orange Gatorade. Because, well, you never know.

CHAPTER TWENTY-TWO

Striking a Pose

The cars that drove by and specifically swerved to splash in the puddles in the gutter to drench us were particularly evil. We had been out there since five in the morning, and for a girl on second shift, who didn't get off of work until 10 p.m. and hadn't seen the morning side of 5 a.m. in a number of years (the evening side of 5 a.m. had been a familiar companion to me due to overtime hours or just being with my Vagabond crew after they had officially shut down for the night), this was quite an achievement for me. I waved my sign and tried to get a chant going, but no one really seemed interested. It wasn't quite the camaraderie I had anticipated, but at least we were all out there together walking the picket line. I often wish I could ask those people in the past who faced far greater difficulties than I what they would do in certain situations, but the fact remains that were they still alive, or could hear me, they too were simply people, trying to do what needed to be done to insure their own lives and livelihoods.

I held a sign against the sun, waved at people driving by, and hoped that this would make a difference. And I was part of a brotherhood (siblinghood, for all its inclusiveness and gender equality, lacks the dramatic flair of its masculine counterpart). It wasn't just the fraternal order of the police that I felt a kinship with; it was the AFL-CIO, Samuel Gompers, the Newsies, the garment factory workers of 1911, and every brave soul who ever stood up and asked for better working conditions and pay so that they might buy food and shelter for themselves and their families.

I realize that the workers of the past had horrific experiences and working conditions that drove them to unionize, and I know that by comparison, we led decadent and easy lives. It wasn't the pay scale that drove this picket, as the media and city government claimed. The problem lay beyond the money and the benefits that clouded the newspaper reports. The city had rejected the use of separate mediation in binding arbitration. The city had said that they would not submit to the findings of the independent mediator that they had hired. They would not allow a contract to be forced upon them. However, the city, under state law, had a right to force a contract upon us. They had the right to say what conditions we had to accept.

I'll be one of the first people to say that the management of the police department needed work. Many of the managers were lazy and greedy and prejudiced. And many were fine upstanding decent human beings. However, this wasn't a contract for the management of the department. This was a contract for the officers on the street and the detectives. This was the contract for the people who solve crimes and run towards bullets when they are fired. This was a contract for men and women who daily risk their lives so that the rest of the city can lie in bed at night without worrying if their houses will be riddled with bullets come morning. These were the people who hunt serial killers, chase down people with guns, and jump into the middle of a gang fight to try to save as many people as possible. These were also the people who work two jobs so that they can afford to send their children to college and perhaps save some money for retirement. These were the people who were possibly going to lose all overtime pay due to new regulations. And all they were asking for was the right to have an independent observer look at both sides and make a decision. They would stand by that decision, whatever it might be. The city council had voted to pay the new city manager over $150,000 a year, plus give him a car, cell phone, and full health care coverage. The council was also in favor of raising sales taxes to fund a new downtown arena, and they were trying to revitalize the city by creating a new water walk along the Arkansas River. What good is a water walk if all it contains are gang hideouts? And what good is a city if it trods upon the rights of the very people it asks to protect it and its citizens?

And so I walked. And waved. And held my sign up for everyone to read. And I remembered the people of years gone by who had also walked and waved and blazed the trail. They were doing what they had to do for their lives and their families. So were we. Would it work? I didn't know. But if we tried and did not succeed, I wasn't going to let anyone call it a failure. Failure was not trying at all.

Six months later, prosecution for the case went smoothly. The medical experts testified to the extent of her injuries and his. I talked about the hairs with the roots and the blood spatter. Defense asked hardly any questions.

The victim, injuries now healed, spoke in a clear calm voice. She identified her attacker and explained that she had gone to the hotel to have sex with him. She thought he was attractive and nice and he had once spoken about finding a nice girl and settling down.

But when they got to the hotel room, he wanted to have anal sex and she refused. She didn't want to do that, she said. She still wanted to have sex with him, but not anal sex.

He grabbed her by the arm and threw her face down on the bed. She couldn't scream and could barely breathe. A pillow had been shoved in her mouth. He had hiked up her skirt and torn her underwear. She felt pressure in her anus and then pain. Horrible pain. Tearing pain.

He still had her arm behind her back and her wrist was hurting too. She thought she heard it crack. He bit her on the shoulder. He flipped her over and began to have "regular" sex with her. She screamed and he punched her in the face at least three times. She tore at his face with her nails. She just wanted to die. And though her voice shook, she spoke clearly and answered the questions.

The defense attorney stepped up to the podium.

CHAPTER TWENTY-THREE
Footloose And Fancy Free

As it turns out, I'm not immune to the CSI effect. Sometimes even I manage to truly believe that things should happen pretty much as they do on a television show that has a monthly budget larger than the yearly one for the Wichita crime lab.

As I stared at the human tibia on the ground in front of me, I immediately thought of the episode where they found one bone fragment out in the Nevada desert and then set up a huge grid search with dozens of policemen who flagged body parts as they came upon them.

When I'd responded to the call that a bone had been found, my first thought was that if I'd been called out on one more bone that turned out to be a deer antler or chicken leg, I would be justified in beating the officers over the head with it and making them do the chicken dance right there on the scene. And when I arrived on the scene, I found myself having to climb a ladder up to a railroad trestle that took me to the other side of the riverbank, where two officers waited in the neck-deep vegetation with what was obviously a human tibia. A right human tibia. Huh, I thought. A human tibia.

Admittedly, this wasn't the most profound of observations, but I was so floored by the idea that the officers had called in a bone that actually turned out to be human, that my brain was forced back into autopilot mode. Luckily, for me autopilot resembles my human osteology textbook, which I had memorized my sophomore year of college because my brain found it amusing to remember useless things like the fact that James Roebling built early suspension bridges and Frederick Olmsted designed Central Park, rather than important things like where I left my keys and how long milk can stay in the refrigerator before it goes bad.

"It's a right human tibia," I told the officers. "The medial malleolus is intact. It looks like a probable male tibia to me, but a forensic anthropologist might be able to give more detail."

The officers looked at me. "You're just here to take pictures and look around," one told me. "We'll get the real diagnosis from the expert."

No one ever says that to Grissom. Then again, Grissom only goes to the most important scenes. It's always a murder, or a sexual assault with lots of blood, or a shooting. I had just come from a sex shop robbery where no one had been injured, and in fact, no one had even been in the store. Sex shop robberies in Wichita were always a bit of a mystery. No one ever saw anything, and no clients were ever actually present during one of these crimes. No, in Wichita, the only two reasons for anyone to be in a sex store were because they needed directions, or they had to use the phone. I had no idea how these megastores stayed in business because no one ever visited them to buy anything. I would pull up to the scene in the clunky blue van, and ask the clerk and any other people if they had seen which door the robber had used, and if anyone noticed if he had been wearing gloves. And the people who were not gainfully employed in the store would widen their eyes and blurt out "I didn't see anything. I was just here to use the phone." I once had a man tell me that this was a matter of life and death and he had to use the phone to call his wife, who would be frantic with worry over his whereabouts. I nodded. Well, sure, if he really needed to use a phone and this was the closest building, then I could certainly understand his reasons for being here. Of course, when his pants started ringing halfway through the explanation, I found his reasoning a little more difficult to buy. "Sir, why don't you take a minute. Your pants are trying to get your attention." I live for moments like that. Moments when I can keep a straight face and say in a perfectly serious tone, as befits a crime scene investigator at a robbery scene, that the person is lying, and I know he's lying, and he knows that I know that he's lying, until we're caught up in an endless loop of knowledge that he can't escape. Kansas and Missouri seemed to have an equal ratio of sex shops and megachurches. I don't know if one has anything to do with the other, but I had some suspicions. The line, "Sir, I don't care if you were looking to buy blow-up dolls, I just want to know if you saw which door the suspect used," has never been uttered on any crime scene TV show. And for that, I feel sorry for the actors. They could use some more comedic writing.

Back with the officers and the tibia, I felt my hackles rise just a bit, which surprised me, as I didn't know I had hackles, or what precisely hackles were, but they rose all the same. It was so tempting to snap back, that—after having endured numerous physical anthropology classes at Columbia, several of which involved final exams where you were presented with a tiny bone fragment and you had to identify it based on various points of identification, involving small holes or bumps or depressions on the bone—I was more than qualified to determine which side of the body a whole tibia came from. Granted, I wasn't a forensic anthropologist, but CSIs have to be trained as generalists in so many different areas that we generally have a grasp on most of the scientific fields. Basics in physics, chemistry, anthropology, biology, and entomology are all necessary.

Instead, I nodded and told the officers to wait by the bone for confirmation from the medical investigator, and I would start looking for other signs of human remains. Of course, this wasn't the Nevada desert. This was the growing season of Wichita, Kansas, and thus the foliage was verdant, thick, and most definitely thriving by the river. There was no way for one person to properly examine the ground. The CSI folks had a flat, dry area and just had to glance around to find their bones. I practically need a machete just to carve a walking path. By the time the medical investigator arrived and commented, unprompted by me, that it was a right tibia and that he was glad the medial malleolus was in place, I was too hot and sweaty to gloat appropriately.

Pat called out the one person with a trained cadaver dog in the area, and we let him get to work. If there were any more parts to the body lying around, the dog would find them. He had a much better chance of locating any evidence than I did, since my sense of smell isn't so great at the best of times, and standing in neck-high foliage wasn't helping my hay fever or olfactory senses any. The dog looked at us, sniffed the bone, and then gazed about the scenery. He glanced back at his handler as if to say, "I can smell five rabbits, a number of squirrels, and a frightened chipmunk within thirty feet of where I'm standing, and you want me to look for a bone with no meat on it??" before starting out down the river. As we waited, Pat told me about how, fifteen years ago at the confluence of the Little and Big Arkansas Rivers, a Red Wing boot was found with the bones of the foot still intact. Five years later, much further south in the river, the other boot and foot bones were discovered. Now we had a tibia that might go with them. We had no idea who this person might be, or if the tibia belonged to the same person as the feet. The feet hadn't looked as though they had been severed prior to death, which meant that a person died, and then somehow, his feet detached from his body. Pat bet money that this tibia belonged to the same person. I pondered this. There are 206 bones in the normal human body. At a rate of one per decade, it would take about two-thousand years for the rest of the body to show up, give or take (as we had the complete foot and that had a lot of bones in it). And while on TV they would do a hunt up and down the river in the department riverboat (yes, they have a riverboat, because they're CSI and they have everything), here in the real world, we didn't have dozens of officers to spare for a hunt, and besides, we also didn't have jurisdiction once we left the Wichita city limits. We would just have to ask neighboring police departments to let us know if they found any body parts, or a body missing a right foot and tibia. The medical investigator left with the bone in hand. The officers wandered off back to their car. The cadaver dog and handler shrugged and gave up. And Pat and I went back across the railroad trestle to the van and drove back to the lab, where I wrote a brief report about the bone, which would get filed in the "Huh. How weird. But nothing more we can do about it now" drawer in my office. Now there's one thing that I've got that they don't have on CSI.

CHAPTER TWENTY-FOUR

Cameron

"Hot or iced?" Pete asked. He already had the box of chai mix and milk out and ready for me to finish the order. "Long Island," I replied. I didn't wait for him to make it but went over to the corner booth and sat. I had not made eye contact with anyone yet. I stared at the table, at the wood grain, and traced the horizontal lines with my fingers. Breathe, I told myself. Breathe. The glass slid over to my hand as I felt Pete slide onto the bench next to me.

"Hey, CSI, want to talk?" I put the red straw in my mouth and drained the glass in one go. Even when worried, Pete made his drinks strong. I coughed a little from the sting of the alcohol, and then slid the glass back. "I need another one." Pete took the glass without a word, got up, and returned a minute later. He slid one glass over to me, and put another one in front of himself. The liquid in my cup was clear. I flicked my eyes over to the one in front of him, which was the proper color for a Long Island iced tea.

"You get the second one after you've finished the water."

"You can't cut me off," I said with mounting anger. "I'm not drunk. I just got off work, and I've only had the one drink."

Pete nodded. "True. But you will be. Laura, in the year you've been coming here, I've seen you have like two rum and Cokes, and those were on separate nights. You have two of these and you'll be porcelain-worship-bound within the hour. Have you had dinner?"

"I don't have to tell you." I wanted him to cut me off, so I would have reason to really fight with him. I needed the outrage. Pete paused.

"Cate! Pita and hummus, and I'm off tonight," he called to the other bartender. She didn't object so I assumed he had some silent communication with her, as well. I hadn't looked up from the table since sitting down. My fingers dug into the fabric of my pants. I grabbed the water and drank it down, and then finished the second

Long Island iced tea.

"I need another one." Pete didn't move.

"You've been here seven minutes," he said quietly. "You've had two drinks that will knock you on your ass in a few more. What happened? You want me to call James?"

I shook my head. I didn't want to see James. I was spoiling for a fight and James deserved better than that. Cate came over with the food and set it down in front of me. Tall, thin, 1920s bob in her dyed black hair and a reach longer than most, she bent over Pete, took my right hand and pried my fingers out of my leg. She placed my hand in Pete's and walked back to the bar to take care of the other customers. I hunched my shoulders but didn't move my hand. I wanted to disappear.

"Laura." Pete said my name insistently and tightened his grip on my fingers. "Laura, honey, what happened?"

I burst into dry sobs, hyperventilating, trying to get air and finding none. When I was eight, I had an asthma attack. It felt as though all the air had left the atmosphere and there was none left for me. No matter what I did, I couldn't breathe. I felt that again. Pete had hold of me in a tight hug. He rocked slightly back and forth while saying "Hey" over and over. I pressed my face into his shoulder.

Wichita has one of the only pediatric trauma units in Kansas. For emergencies in the surrounding farm communities and small towns, the hospital helicopter flies over, picks up the injured, and gets them back to the city and help as fast as they can. And on farms, there can be some pretty nasty incidents. Children and farm equipment just don't mix at times. Often the children just want to emulate their parents, and forbidden machinery offers them the chance to do that, coupled with the excitement of disobedience. When accidents happen, there are times when we're called out and times when things are so clear cut, the doctors feel comfortable listing the cause of the injury or the manner of death as accidental. In this case, they felt comfortable enough listing Cameron's as intentional injury, and if he died, they would list it as a homicide.

The case had started five days ago, my "Monday" but Friday for most people. They had called for a lab in the hospital for pictures, and time was of the essence. I hopped in the van and immediately got beeped to go to a private channel.

"Laura, it's a certain child abuse case. Kid might not make it. Detectives are at the scene, but they can't find the weapon. Looks like a stomping but no shoes match. Take a look at the pattern, would you, and see if you can make sense of it."

I sighed. Human horrors in five sentences or less. Wichita detectives would win that game show hands down.

At the hospital, I found Cameron in the NICU, Natal Intensive Care Unit. He was six months old. A tube down his throat looked almost like a pacifier except it made a whooshing sound every few seconds, making Cameron's chest rise and fall. He wasn't breathing on his own. He was perfect, ten fingers, ten toes, the wispy blond hair that only babies ever have. The pattern of red and white dots on his forehead confused me. They were regular, repetitive. But so tiny. This wasn't a shoe pattern, I was sure of it. I brushed back his hair with a latex-gloved hand and, as gently as possible, placed a small metric scale by the pattern injury. I bent low, keeping the camera lens perpendicular to the scale, and began my wound photograph series. Midrange, close up. Without scale and with scale. Where had I seen those dots before? They looked so familiar. I knew them. I knew those dots. I stopped by the nurses' station to get some data for my report. I didn't need to know his condition, just a police case number. The rest of my report would read that photographs only were requested, and then a photography log, with the photographs attached. I drummed my fingers on the countertop as the duty nurse flipped through the chart and stared at the flickering computer screen and the computer speakers next to the screen. The tiny dots of the computer speakers … I clicked on my radio.

"Check the computer speakers. It looks like computer speaker dots." The detective swore. I wasn't sure if I was supposed to wait for confirmation or not, but no other calls had come in, so I went back to Cameron's room.

His eyelashes were so small and fine and his fingernails were so little. He looked serene and wise and frail. I took off my gloves and put his hand around one of my fingers. He felt warm but didn't react. My radio crackled to life, and I jumped as if afraid the sound would wake him.

"Thanks, Laura. Two hairs and a small blood stain on the left speaker. Can you do follow up over the next couple days to see if any bruising comes up? Just do one report at the end."

I hadn't said anything else to Pete after my initial outburst, but at least it let the tears come, and the air seemed to return to the area around me. To his credit, Pete hadn't even hesitated in his rocking motion or soothing noises.

I heard a clink of glasses and felt the table shift slightly as two more people entered the booth. Irini was about to leave for Iraq in a week. I didn't know him all that well, but he was a Vagabond regular who spent his time sketching the patrons and bartenders on napkins. I had several of his sketches of me framed on the walls of my apartment. He always chose to draw me when I was looking down at my journal, writing about the day's events.

Once, he drew me as I was writing about him drawing me. Jason was about to enter school as a pharmacy technician, and better yet, he played a decent hand of Crazy Eights.

A chair scraped as Bill pulled one over to the head of the table. Bill was the resident computer genius who could always fix the Internet connection at the Vagabond computer whenever it caught a virus. We suspected that someone was looking at some rather disreputable Internet sites, but no one ever complained and I hadn't noticed anything odd in the user history when I used the computer.

I looked up at the concerned faces surrounding me and realized that the Vagabond regulars had formed a human shield around me. Curious onlookers would only see the backs of people's heads, unless they stood right over us, and I had a feeling Cate would have something to say about any actions which remotely resembled that. The family was closing ranks to outsiders.

The purpling around Cameron's right eye was visible the next day. It was bluish purple, which meant it would turn darker as time went by. It ringed the socket, as if a beauty school freshman had taken eye shadow and decided to color in below as well as above the eye. It was darkest by his nose. A small bruise on his temple was also beginning to form. I photographed it with and without scale, as I was supposed to do. I also sat and held his hand again, which I was not supposed to do, but who was going to stop me? It seemed wrong that there were no grieving parents here. Where were his relatives? Where were the people who were supposed to care about him? I sat there and told him a Russian fairy tale I had read once, about three brothers who went off in search of their fortunes. The youngest received a magic cloak, boots that could travel seven leagues in one step, and a ring that would make him invisible. Using these, he saved a princess from an ogre, married the girl, and inherited the kingdom. I may have gotten some of the details wrong, and I couldn't remember what the other two brothers did, or how their destinies worked out, but I didn't think Cameron would mind.

The next morning, before work, I went out and bought a small yellow teddy bear for his bed. The purple around his eye and on his temple were now fully developed. They were a deep purple, but the blue was gone. It would start to fade to green and yellow in a day or two. I asked a nurse to lift him up or roll him so I could examine his back and make sure I hadn't missed anything on his back, legs, arms, or neck. We didn't see any other sign of trauma, though the MRI and CAT scan showed brain swelling, detached retinas, and no brain activity.

I told him the story of Hansel and Gretel, who went into the forest with only breadcrumbs to leave a trail to find their way back. They came to a gingerbread house, where they met a kindly old woman who took them in, and loved them, and fed them vegetables as well as gingerbread. When their parents came looking for them, frantic with worry because they loved their children, the children's father recognized her as his long-lost mother and they all lived happily ever after. Cameron had enough trouble in his life; I didn't want to tell him there were more evil people in the world.

The fourth day of my acquaintance with Cameron I brought a music box that played "When You Wish Upon a Star." I told him of Pinocchio, and Geppetto, and that Geppetto's wish for a son was so strong that the blue fairy granted the wish and Pinocchio came to life. He was excited by the world around him, but even though he loved his father, he was still made of wood and so went on a journey to figure out how to be a real boy. He was swallowed by a whale, but Jiminy Cricket, whom I had forgotten to mention earlier but had been with Pinocchio the whole time, helped him build a fire and the whale sneezed him out onto the shore where Geppetto found him. The blue fairy came and made Pinocchio a real boy and they lived happily ever after.

The nurse promised to wind the music box a couple of times a day. His bruises were now purple with just a touch of green. He still never reacted when I held his hand. I didn't use gloves anymore to put a scale on his forehead for the photographs.

The alcohol hit me after Pete had been holding me for about twenty minutes or so. I hadn't eaten that day and I wasn't used to drinking so it didn't take much to push me from buzzed to completely drunk. I couldn't stand up even if I wanted to and the world had taken on a counterclockwise spin. Irini kept blurring into Jason, and Bill seemed to have a twin brother next to him. I told Pete this and he said something unintelligible to Bill, who promptly got up to let Pete slide out, dragging me with him. I didn't really want to go anywhere, but he pulled me out and with Bill on one side and Pete on the other, they half-walked, half-carried me to the bathroom. Pete flipped the sign to "Occupied" and all three of us went in. An insistent knock at the door and Cate's voice made Pete open it up once. Cate had a penchant for the jelly bracelets that were so popular in the 1980s and always had five or six on her wrists. I was dimly aware as she took one off and pulled my hair into a ponytail and then left to get back to the bar. I heard her voice call out that the women's restroom was broken and that everyone would just have to use the men's room. Pete rubbed my back and gently lowered me in front of the toilet just in time for a clear stream of fluid to gush from my mouth. It burned as much coming up as it had going down. The world seemed very hazy around the edges.

Tuesday dawned with nothing more on my agenda than to think of something else to brighten up Cameron's room. I decided it needed a little visual stimulation and a bright blanket might be nice to look at as well as touch. I wanted something soft, with maybe a picture of an airplane or a boat. I loved playing with toy boats as a child, and it seemed the right sort of thing. After a fruitless hunt for something suitable at two of the independent baby and children's stores, I told myself to stop being stymied by my overly developed sense of morality and go to Wal-Mart, which has every product known to man. I gritted my teeth and drove over there, only to find the perfect soft boat blanket within thirty seconds of walking into the store. You had to say this, everyone jokes they're an evil empire, but they really do have a fabulous selection. I barely checked into the lab that day before heading out to show Cameron his blanket. I hadn't mentioned any of this to the other lab personnel because I wasn't sure they would understand, and I didn't want a lecture about shirking work in favor of being in the hospital. I had taken other calls during the week, but hadn't written up my reports on them yet. I was last up for a call that night, and with a full staff of all five of us on shift, and me technically taking a call to go take pictures of Cameron, I knew I would most likely be free for the rest of the night.

When I arrived at the hospital, the nurse on call asked me to let her know when I had finished taking my photographs. Since no one had asked me that before, I was curious as to the change in protocol. What was different about today? She sighed.

"The state got permission to take him off life support when you're finished today."

I felt the floor tip slightly. "What?"

"He won't develop new visible injuries and there's no brain activity. The doctors and detectives and courts all agree that we don't need to prolong things any further."

I nodded. Yes, it made sense to not prolong things. After all, he was in pain. He must be in pain. We should let him go. We should let him be at peace.

I walked into the room and put a scale on Cameron's forehead. There was definitely a green tinge to the edges. The red and white pattern of dots that had tattled on the computer speaker was fading. His chest rose and fell with the machinery. I took my photographs. It was better this way, I told myself. I sat down and held his hand. I told him about the little engine that could, and how he really did make it up the hill, with the cheers and support of the local townspeople and all the other train cars doing their best to help him along. I wound up the music box. I told him about Jack and his beanstalk, and how he climbed up to the clouds where he found a very nice giant and his wife who invited him in for dinner. After a lovely meal, the giant mentioned that he had a harp that sang and that it was keeping him awake at night and he would appreciate it if Jack would take it off his hands. The giant would give Jack a lot of gold for his trouble. Jack agreed and the gold helped him set up a prosperous farm, and the giant and his wife had Jack and his mother over for dinner once a week, since they were a little lonely, being the only people living up in the clouds.

I told him about King Arthur and Merlin, and how they set up a round table to show that no one was any better than anyone else, and how they convinced everyone else in the land to join them, and that was how England became the most powerful nation on the planet for a long time, because all the people worked together and helped one another. And that Arthur and Guinevere lived happily ever after, and Lancelot married Guinevere's long-lost sister, and the four of them would go for picnics in the woods.

I told him about Robin Hood, who won archery contests, and who had a misunderstanding with Prince James, and so he and his friends went camping in the woods for a while and they hunted lots of deer and gave them to the poor people who weren't such good shots with bows and arrows. And then Prince James's brother, King Richard, came home from his trip overseas and set things right, and Robin Hood and his friends came back to their homes and everyone lived happily ever after.

The nurse looked in several times and then brought a chair over to the corner of the room. I didn't want the stories to end and I still had two hours left on my shift, but I was running out of stories that didn't center around a princess pricking her finger or sleeping for a long time. I wanted to tell Cameron stories that little boys would like. And as soon as I told the medical staff that I was done, they would take him off life support. As long as I could keep the stories going, as long as I wasn't done, then he would keep living. I couldn't let myself stop.

The nurse cleared her throat and I started to look up with a glare, but she began a tale of a little boy lion who was supposed to be king one day, but he got lost in the jungle. Luckily, he came across a friendly meerkat and a warthog who helped him find food and eventually got him back home where his mother and best friend greeted him and he became king of the jungle.

That reminded me of the little boy named Tarzan who washed up on the shores of Africa and lived happily ever after with the gorillas who took him in. The nurse looked over at me.

"Maybe just one more." She gave a little encouraging nod and left the room, with just one quick glance back at me. I took both of Cameron's hands in mine and told him of Peter Pan, who was a little boy who didn't know who his mother was, but he found Wendy and lots of friends, and they all went to live together with the Indians and pirates (who were good and kind, and maybe just a little scary but it was only for show) in Never Never Land. Peter Pan, who never had anything bad happen to him that he couldn't handle, and of course, who never grew up. I pushed back his hair and kissed the side of his head that wasn't bruised, and told the nurse that the crime lab had finished its job with Cameron. I called in to the lab that I was taking an hour of sick leave, and drove straight to the Vagabond. For the first time, I showed up there still in uniform.

I woke up in the Vagabond's back room on the couch. My head felt stuffed with cotton, and my mouth tasted as though I had somehow eaten rotten cheese the previous night. There was a toothbrush and toothpaste on the table in front of me, and I saw a sheet tacked up over the entrance to the room.

The Vagabond was a coffee shop and a bar, and thus opened up at 5 a.m. every morning and closed at 2 a.m. the following day. I could hear the clink of glasses and the tinkle of the bells at the door to signal that morning customers were getting their coffee on the way to work. I walked slightly unsteadily to the bathroom, toothpaste and brush in hand, and scrubbed away the taste and smell of the previous night. As I came back out, I saw a pair of pants, a shirt, bra, and underwear folded on a chair. They were all clothing items from my closet. None of the Vagabond people had ever been to my apartment, but they all knew where I lived. Since the clothing matched, I guessed that Cate had picked them out. My keys were on top of the pile. There was also a note saying that Pyewacket had been fed.

My hands shook, and I remembered Cameron. I should have thanked everyone for all their concern and help. I should have felt gratitude welling up inside. But I remembered Cameron and how I helped to kill him. I got dressed, walked up to the bar, and ordered a rum and Coke.

CHAPTER TWENTY-FIVE

Campfire Tales

The cows lowed menacingly. "Holy crap, Laura, I think they're trying to flank us!" James and I slowly backed away toward the barbed wire fence we had come through just a few minutes previously. I no longer cared if I stepped in something nasty, and kept my eyes firmly on the advancing cattle. Their pace quickened. I saw more appearing over the ridge and James fumbled for his gloves to hold the fence wire up for me to scramble beneath. The cows were coming.

After Cameron, Wichita became a prison for me. My crime scene van was a mobile jail cell, taking me from one scene of anguish to another. I drove to scenes where mothers had accidentally killed their children, where cars ran over toddlers, and where eight-year-olds on ATVs tore their heads open on low-hanging branches. There was an aura of death around me that the Vagabond couldn't dispel. I worked scenes, I went out to dinner with friends, and I hugged my cat a lot, but instead of participating, it felt as though I were a spectator in my own life, watching my body go through the motions. In desperation, I started hunting for another job. Any job. I looked at teaching jobs at local colleges, but none provided health insurance. I thought of writing a newspaper column, but rent and bills seemed to make that impossible. Staying in Wichita seemed less of an option, except for my friends, and James. James somehow managed to keep me smiling through it all. He had the uncanny knack of knowing exactly when I might begin to sink into despair, and he'd suddenly look up and say, "A witch doctor decontaminated the house I'm building today." What? It was enough to disrupt my self-pity moment and cause me to look up in bewilderment.

"Yeah," he told me. "Apparently, I used some really unlucky piece of wood in the doorframe, and this Chinese family needed to have the evil wood spirits driven out."

Evil wood spirits? I went from cracking the first grin in many days to doubled over with laughter as he described the outfit, the stick shaking, the chanting of the Chinese witch doctor. His eyes glinted at me and he pulled me in for a hug.

"You're beautiful all the time, but especially when you smile."

I hugged him back hard and didn't want to leave the warmth of his arms. We stayed that way for a while until he finally regretfully pulled away to stop the pasta from boiling over on the stove.

The job interview in Portland, Oregon, was a secret I didn't even tell Patti about. I was flying out on a Wednesday morning, interviewing on Thursday morning, and flying back Thursday night in time for my shift on Friday afternoon. It was a laboratory job—no more crime scenes if I got it. Just the safety of a lab. No parental tears or crying girlfriends. Just pure evidence. Stains on fabric and broken glass. It sounded so clean and detached and just what I needed. I checked into the hotel and opened the letter James had given me. It wasn't a long one, just a reminder that when I got back, we were going camping and that he loved me. He wished me luck.

They say that if you love someone, then you need to let them go to see if they'll come back to you. Was he letting me go to see if I returned? I wondered. I hung up my suit and sprayed some anti-wrinkle chemical on it. (I've never owned an iron and wouldn't know what to do with one if the hotel provided one.) Portland looked exciting and not nearly as rainy as I had anticipated.

As I left to go check out the city, I did my mental check for my wallet, keys, and cell phone and headed out into the sunshine, only to realize as the door clicked shut behind me and that I had checked for my normal keys, not the room keycard. I panicked. Oh dear god, for as long as I could remember my father had always, always, asked me if I had the hotel key on any vacation. He would ask me that when he came to visit me in college. He asked me that in a voice that bespoke of dire consequences if I locked myself out. All of my things were in the room. What was I going to do? I would have to leave my suit behind, and live in Portland since my plane tickets were still in that room. How could I have been so stupid? What was I to do? As I raced down to the lobby, a million ruinous thoughts crossed my mind. The situation was hopeless. My father was going to have to rescue me, if I worked up the courage to call him. I didn't even have my rental car keys with me! How would I get to my interview?

So it turns out that when you lock yourself out of your hotel room, the kindly front desk people give you another key. (I just wanted you to know, Dad.)

The interview went well. I nearly laughed when they asked me if I could handle evidence that smelled of death. I, Laura Merz, who had worn the skin of a dead man to get fingerprints, be put off by the smell of death? Never! I even explained the icky bug dance to them, and they all laughed in recognition. The lab personnel were close to my age and friendly, and the facilities were beautiful. But in my mind, I just wanted to get back home to James. My crime scene van was a jail cell, but James was the warden, and he breathed freedom back into me each night. We had camping to do. In truth, I had never been camping, unless that one time back at Indian Princesses counted, where I slept in a cabin and caught a fish, which so traumatized me that I cried until my dad threw it back in the water. So this would be a new experience. I worried about toilets. No one would ever classify me as high maintenance, but I do like clean bathroom facilities. James had warned of a lack of any sort of toilets other than what Mother Nature provided. He was trying to keep me occupied. Trying to keep me interested and upbeat, because he could see Cameron in my eyes if I was left alone to think for too long. He didn't know I was seeing Cameron, because I hadn't explained it all to him, but he knew that in my line of work, sometimes I saw things that shouldn't be seen. And I loved him for that. For not needing an explanation and loving me anyway.

We drove out to the Flint Hills a week after I locked myself out of the Portland hotel. In the midst of the low rolling landscape, he stopped the truck and pitched a tent big enough for two. A few sticks and a lighter started our campfire, and once the sleeping bags and lawn chairs were unloaded, James looked at me and shrugged.

"That's really about it. Now, it's just sit back and relax."

He sounded a little sheepish, as though apologizing for the lack of excitement. After all, I was a New York girl, and still an anomaly in his Kansas lifestyle. He was worried I'd find it all too... country. We sat in the lawn chairs and watched the stars come out. I had read once that you knew you were in love with someone if you could sit quietly beside him and not feel a need to fill the silence. We held hands and didn't say much for about an hour. James pointed to the sky.

"That's the Milky Way." I goggled a bit at the bright line crossing the stars. For all my love of science, for all my stargazing, never once had the light pollution of the East Coast or even Wichita allowed me to see our own galaxy. And there were so many stars. How had the Greeks even seen the constellations when the stars filled the sky like that? The night sky isn't black when all the lights are out. It's a pearly white with bits of darkness. And I never knew that until James. When we went to sleep that night, he apologized again for the lack of excitement. And I looked into his eyes, stopping only to once more feel a pang of envy at his ridiculously long eyelashes, thinking that he was all the excitement I ever wanted.

"You're the first girl I've ever brought out here," James told me when we got up the next morning. He was already cooking breakfast over the fire, and I grabbed my camera to commemorate the event. There were people back in New York who wouldn't believe I had been on a real camping trip. Of course, thanks to an industrial-sized bladder and sheer willpower, I hadn't yet tried to figure out how to go to the bathroom, but other than that one minor inconvenience, I was enjoying every second. But the pronouncement puzzled me. This was bliss. James had been married before. How had he never brought his ex-wife out here when they were still together? He shrugged when I asked.

"She just never showed an interest in coming out here."

I squeezed his shoulder. Somehow, I couldn't help thinking, I'd be interested in being wherever he was.

"Hey, after breakfast, you want to take a look at the field to the side of the lake? It looked like a nice view."

As we set off, we didn't know that the particular field we were about to explore was populated with cows. Hungry cows. And the only humans they saw were the ones who brought them food. As we wandered past the barbed wire fence, their heads perked up. City girl that I am, I was a little nervous, but with James with me, I knew it would be all right.

"Are those cows coming toward us?" James asked me. I looked up in alarm. Sure enough, the bovine herd had moved closer and was now eyeing us with interest. We were moving farther from the fence line and into their territory. I sensed trouble brewing.

"Hey, maybe we should go back…" James scoffed at the suggestion. "I'm not going to let a bunch of menacing cows scare us off," he told me. I nodded. James knew what he was doing. He was a Wichita boy. By now the herd had grown to several dozen cows. The lead one let out a loud MMOOOO and set off for us at a fast clip. James froze.

"Okay, you know, we should get out of here." He backpedaled quickly, keeping a hand on my arm to make sure I was moving along with him. As we backtracked, the herd, sensing the humans who would feed them were leaving, picked up the pace. In the mad scramble back under the fence, I scraped my leg and tore my shirt sleeve a little. James shook his head.

"We got chased away by cows! Cows! What the hell?! But damn it, they were Marauding Cows!" he exclaimed. For one brief second I thought my bladder control would fail me, but as we leaned on each other for support from the laughter, I knew that even if it did, it wouldn't matter. James wouldn't care—he might tease me about it privately, but he loved me and that was the important thing. That and we were on the other side of the fence from the cows.

CHAPTER TWENTY-SIX
Brushing Up on My Technique

One of the more overlooked tools in a crime scene kit is the lowly toothbrush. It's ever so important for gently brushing away grime and grit from in between window sills and metal grates. It helps get filings away from tool marks and allows me to save my much more fragile fingerprint powder brushes for actually looking for fingerprints. I had just donated the last new toothbrush that I had brought with me to Kansas to my crime scene kit, when tragedy struck. Normally, I would not expect Pyewacket knocking my toothbrush into the toilet to cause a mental meltdown, but that was before I had to purchase a new toothbrush. You see, years ago, when I lived at home, normal rectangular-headed toothbrushes would magically appear in the bathroom linen closet with surprising regularity. The tooth fairy would bring them in the night and leave them there for me to take to college, grad school, and Wichita with me. I would restock whenever I went home, seeing as how the tooth fairy always knew when a new toothbrush would be needed. So I never paid much attention to the variety of toothbrushes available to me.

The first toothbrush innovation I really remember was the switch from the rectangular head to the diamond head. I remember the commercial well. The poor diamond-headed toothbrush was laughed at mercilessly by the rectangular-headed toothbrush as they sat in their holder in the bathroom. The diamond-headed one got depressed even though he KNEW that his unique shape helped clean teeth better. (I don't remember why it helped clean teeth better, but the toothbrush said so, so it must be true. After all, one doesn't want to mess with talking toothbrushes.) Luckily, the rectangular toothbrush was thrown away, and "Peggy" moved in next door. I specifically remember this part. She was a diamond-headed toothbrush who moved her bristles in such a way as to simulate fluttering eyelashes. To this day I don't know how she did that, because I actually have eyelashes and I can't flutter them at all, and yet this hussy of a toothbrush managed to do it without eyes, eyelids, or lashes. So everyone lived happily ever after and the moral of the story is, buy a diamond-headed toothbrush. (I don't remember the brand, but I remember the girl toothbrush's name... which shows how my brain picks weird things to keep in it.)

Then came the Reach toothbrush. It had an angled neck. This was useful to clean those hard-to-reach back teeth, according to the commercial. In fact, the only two choices you had for good dental hygiene were to buy a Reach toothbrush or get a flip-top head. I really really wanted a flip-top head. I was about eight and thought that a flip-top head would make me popular at all sleepovers, and if you've ever been an eight-year-old, you'll know that I was probably right. However, apparently flipping your head open was not as easy as it appeared in the cartoon in the commercial. So I was forced to decide that the Reach toothbrush was the only way to keep my teeth healthy. Not that we ever used those, mind you. We used a regular, rectangular-headed, straight-necked toothbrush, by god, and we liked it!

(As a side note, doesn't anyone else find it fishy that the toothbrush commercials always use a cartoon to show how well their toothbrushes work? Wow! That toothbrush must be good because the animator stopped drawing the plaque on the teeth!)

So when I went to Walgreens to pick up a new toothbrush, I was overcome with the innovations in toothbrushes since I had paid attention to the commercials. There were diamond heads, angled necks, spin brushes, time release color bristles to show when a new toothbrush was needed, easy-grip... The list goes on. I stared at the array before me in wonder and befuddlement. I mean, how many different types of toothbrush do we need? Have my teeth been rotting away in my head because my old toothbrush didn't rotate? Isn't that sort of what my hand motions were doing with my old rectangular-headed toothbrush? Isn't that why the dentist recommended moving my hand in small circles near the gum line when I brushed? If I had had the easy-grip toothbrush, would Pyewacket have gotten a better hold on it as he batted it around, and therefore not knocked it into the toilet? And why did these toothbrushes all cost as much as the GDP of Burkina Faso?

I made the mistake of looking confused while in the toothbrush aisle, which brought the friendly pharmacist over. The friendly pharmacist asked if he could assist me. He had never done such a thing before, but I put that down to the new cleavage-enhancing bra that I was trying out. Turns out that it enhances not only cleavage, but also customer service. I mentioned the variety of toothbrushes at my disposal, and he then said the most horrifying sentence ever uttered in a Walgreens dental care aisle: "What bristle hardness do you prefer?"

Bristle hardness?! What now?! It turns out that every last one of those toothbrushes comes in not only a remarkable array of colors, but also different bristle hardnesses. Did I prefer a firmer bristle or a gentler one? Normally, I don't have these sorts of discussions with a man until the fourth or fifth date, but here it was, in the Walgreens dental care aisle. I had no idea what bristle hardness I preferred. I longed for the magical tooth fairy toothbrushes. The rectangular-headed, straight-necked, hard to grip, non-rotating, normal bristle firmness toothbrushes of yore. Oh, where had they gone?

As I cast about for a suitable answer to the bristle firmness question, my eye fell on a beautiful sight. I swear, a shaft of fluorescent light descended to the dental care aisle, leading me out of troubled waters and into safe territory. A chorus of white-toothed dental hygienists came from above! There, next to the toothbrush display, was my toothpaste—on sale—and with each box they included a FREE toothbrush! Suddenly, the answer seemed so simple. Get the free toothbrush, Laura! Get the free one! I thought the voice came from above somewhere, but in fact I was actually chanting it out loud, making the friendly pharmacist very uncomfortable. I grabbed the box and fled to the counter, paid, and vaulted into my car. When I got home I contemplated my free toothbrush. It had a wavy head, a curved neck, an easy grip, and was the shade of Pepto Bismol. It was the most beautiful sight I had beheld that day.

A man walks into a bar. He's nicely dressed and has a decently expensive watch on his wrist. He sits there for a little while drinking his beer and checking out the pool tables. He comes here often to drink and play pool and socialize. When a spot opens up, another man grabs a pool cue and asks the guy if he's up for a game. The man agrees and they play a round, each buys a round of drinks, and they play one more game before the first man decides to call it a night. The two men shake hands and the first man leaves. The second man follows soon after, and jogs a bit to catch up to the first man, who stops, recognizing him as the person from the bar. Before the first man knows what happened, the second man has his arm twisted behind his back and grabs his wallet. As he keeps hold of the first man's arm, he tells him to give him the watch as well. The first man does it, and the second man runs off with the wallet and watch. The police are called, take a description, interview the bar patrons to see if anyone knows the person, and set out looking for him. When they locate the perpetrator, they take him into custody even though he doesn't have the watch or wallet on him.

Now, change the scenario. Instead of the first person being a man, she's now a woman. And instead of a robbery, the second man raped her. When the first case goes to court, no defense attorney in the world would dare suggest that the victim offered to give the defendant his wallet and watch. No defense attorney would care about how much alcohol the victim drank. No defense attorney would dare suggest that the victim led the suspect on by buying him a round of drinks and playing pool with him.

But in the second case, a defense attorney will suggest that the woman wanted to have sex with the suspect. Why else would she have played pool with him? Why else would she have bought him a round of drinks? Why else would she have stopped and waited as he jogged toward her in the street? The suspect said it was her idea to have sex in the alleyway, and the defense attorney will make that argument.

We are harder on rape victims than we are on any criminals. We pay lip service to "no means no" and "a woman can change her mind at any time," but the police will ask the bar patrons if she was flirting with the suspect. The police will ask how much she had to drink. The defense attorney will bring up the point that she was wearing thong underwear. She was a regular at the bar. She was trolling for sex. No one asks the man who was robbed what sort of underwear he was wearing or if he was flashing around too much cash in a bad neighborhood. And no one blames him for being robbed. Even if he had left his car unlocked with the keys in the ignition and the robber had stolen it, it would not make it any less of a car theft.

But somehow, if the woman was wearing a thong, it's less of a rape. If she accepted a drink from a man, or if she wore a short skirt, or if she flirted with him and others at the bar, if she danced, if she was drunk, if she was alone, if she had on too much makeup, if her hair was up, if her hair was down, or if she had on a shirt that showed too much cleavage, it makes it less of a rape. Or not a rape at all. At least, in the eyes of the twelve people who have to decide that fact.

CHAPTER TWENTY-SEVEN

The Heat Of the Night

Have you ever had a burglary where that pesky home invader just brings you lots of presents and leaves them about your house? I don't mean little insignificant gifts, but rather, large expensive gifts, like stolen computers. Or toaster ovens. Or bright blue, strawberry-flavored dildos. Because Wichita seemed to have an overabundance of gift-giving burglars. This generally complicates a crime scene, and I really didn't need a complicated scene that day. James and I were supposed to meet for a late-night drink, followed by my first overnight stay at his house. He had been at mine plenty of times, but somehow, I had never stayed with him and he wanted to rectify that immediately. When the call came in at 9:30, I prayed it would be an easy one.

During a burglary scene, I always have the homeowner do a walkthrough with me, to show me the areas of the house that have been disturbed in some way, so I know what and where to fingerprint. In this particular case, I noticed the excess of religious iconography all around me. The Virgin Marys and crucifixes almost obscured the walls. The modest dress and downcast, demure eyes of the homeowner spoke of her modesty and piety. The victim and I came to the bedroom (where the officer had already told me that nothing had been touched) and I barely glanced in, ready to move on to the next room. The victim stood in the doorway, transfixed. She had forgotten that she had not put her toys away. Not her Barbies or domino set—no, she had forgotten to put her adult toys away. Now, I don't really care what people have in their houses. Sure, I saw the toys, but as long as it's not illegal and the burglar didn't touch it, it doesn't concern me. But it sure concerned her. She didn't want me to think she was a pervert. No. She was a perfectly chaste virginal creature who once heard someone mention something about procreation, but she didn't know how it was done. Something to do with eggs, perhaps. She looked at me with panic in her eyes and averred, "The burglar brought those!"

This is not the thing to say to me. Because I'm a crime scene investigator, and now, instead of breezing by this room with one quick overall photograph, I have to go into the room, take close-ups of the items brought in and left by the burglar, collect said items, and attempt to fingerprint them. I had one woman claim that burglars left a large quantity of stolen computer equipment in her garage that night. When I moved the monitors in question, rings of dust showed them to have been there for a bit longer than the hour she was claiming. I once had a woman tell me that a residential robber brought her neighbor's toaster oven with him and left it in her kitchen. I had to collect and fingerprint all those items. And again, I didn't really want to do all that with a bright blue dildo. So I asked her, "The burglar brought those items?"

She nodded. I tried again. "The burglar brought and left a bright blue dildo on your bed?"

She again gave me an affirmative.

It seemed the burglar had also brought the other FIVE bright blue dildos on the floor, and had thoughtfully covered them with strawberry-flavored jelly for her future enjoyment. The burglar had also very thoughtfully stacked the boxes for these items in her bedroom closet.

This seemed like, perhaps, rather a waste of time when one is attempting to ransack a house. I thought I better make sure.

"There are empty jelly packages here in the trash can. So what you're telling me is that some crazed individual broke your kitchen window, climbed through the broken glass, carried six boxes of bright blue dildos and strawberry-flavored jelly into the house, came upstairs to your bedroom, opened the dildo boxes, took them out of the boxes, opened the jelly packages, put the jelly on the dildos, placed them around your bedroom, stacked the boxes in your closet, ran out of the room and down the stairs, grabbed your TV in the kitchen by the broken window, and left the same way he entered."

She nodded, eyes wide and innocent. "Yes, and if there are any porn tapes in the TV cabinet, the burglar left those too."

I was beginning to feel a bit skeptical of her story, but she was unshakable. She didn't even know what a dildo was, and she certainly would never have one in her house. I wondered if it would make any difference to her if I told her that quite honestly, my opinion of her improved considerably when I saw the dildos. I was happy she had a life outside of religion. But she didn't seem like the type to discuss this sort of thing rationally. I went outside and called James.

"Listen, I'm probably going to be late tonight, but trust me, the story is totally worth it."

And so I photographed and collected six bright blue dildos, six strawberry-flavored jelly packets, and six dildo boxes. And I checked them for fingerprints. I am not a religious person, but if there is an afterlife, I do hope the person who invented latex gloves is happy there. I don't really care where the inventor of the dildo is, so long as he isn't doing anything illegal in my sight or claiming that forgers signed his name to the patent after burglars left that invention on his worktable.

I made it to James's house around midnight, to find the lights off and the house quiet, and I nearly turned back around to go home. But his words earlier in the night stopped me.

"Laura, I don't care how late it is. Just promise you'll come by. I'll leave the front door unlocked for you."

I loved living in a place where people could leave their front doors unlocked while they slept. Wichita still had that small-town magic, even if I did see mostly the seedier side of the city.

I crept in through the dark, trying not to make a sound. After pulling my toothbrush out from my bag, and peeking into the bedroom to see James fast asleep on his stomach, eyelashes fluttering in dreams ever so slightly, I made my way to the bathroom. He had left me a note by the sink. A scrap of paper held down by the toothpaste—"I'm so glad you're here." Tears sprang up. I loved him. And he loved me. The words had been said, but it was the atmosphere that was more important. It was here around us. For the first time, I imagined growing old with someone. As I slid between the sheets, he muttered and rolled over. I kissed his back, between his shoulder blades, put my arms around him, and drifted off to sleep, smiling.

CHAPTER TWENTY-EIGHT
Hanging By a Thread

How old does one have to be to feel infinite sadness? Before whatever sorrows a person may have experienced have weighed him down to such an extent that drowning seems preferable to fighting the current? How old do you have to be before struggling against the odds has weakened you to the point of exhaustion, and death seems a relief rather than the enemy?

I had a late call over the radio one July night. I could have left it for third shift, but it had been a slow month, so I decided to take the call myself rather than pass the buck. It was going to be a relatively easy scene. Attempted suicides usually are deceptively simple. The person who tried to kill himself isn't there, having been taken to the hospital, so I generally just photograph the scene, take some measurements, and collect whatever he used to try to end his life.

I drove down the road, searching for the flashing red and blue strobe effects that tell me when I've found the right house. Bangs and crashes shook my van as I climbed out of it, green and yellow adding to the cacophony of colors. Wichitans nearby were giving the Fourth an early sendoff with homemade rockets and fireworks. I only heard every other word the officer spoke. I got the basics. The victim had attempted to hang herself. Her father had been drinking and was passed out on the couch when her younger brother tried to get help. A neighbor had come to the rescue. She had used a tan belt.

It was enough to get started. I photographed. I photographed the beer cans outside the house. I photographed the beer cans in the trashcan in the kitchen. I photographed the beer cans in the bathroom. I photographed the door to her room. She shared it with her younger brothers and sisters. It was such a small room. Ten feet wide, eight feet long. Three beds and a dresser. A pink fairy tale castle blocked the north half of the room from the south. Her younger sister was three-years-old. I could picture it happening. A tan belt, looped over one of the red hooks in the ceiling. Why were there such large hooks in the ceiling? Why did she lean forward? Her brother told the officers that she leaned over the edge of the bed, her arms dangling down. He became frightened when she started foaming at the mouth. I measured the room, the hooks, and the belt. I searched for anything else that could have been used, in case I had picked up the wrong belt. I noticed one of the metal fastenings on the belt had been broken off. It was lying on the bed. A sign of force that indicated I had the right weapon. Weapons of mass destruction. How much mass made her up? Can a belt be considered a weapon like that?

I collected the belt. It fastened with two hooks, one of which was broken off. The other hook lay on the top bunk of the bunk beds, under one of the red hooks in the ceiling. Why were there such large hooks in the ceiling above the bed? The blanket was pulled up under the pillow. Hospital corners on a top bunk. I can't even keep my sheet tucked under my mattress. I measured the hooks. Five inches long. Forty-four inches apart. Thirty-nine inches above the mattress. The tape measure slithered over the walls, a snake encircling the scene of despair. I envisioned an apple tree growing here. The place of knowledge. Of good and evil. How must it feel to eat an apple and suddenly know of evil and pain and anguish and shame? How must it feel to have your protector turn you away because you know of these things? I think the miracle of Genesis is that Adam and Eve didn't kill themselves before or after they were thrown out of the garden. How devastating that knowledge must have been. Did this girl have her own apple? The thing that gave her knowledge that the world is always imperfect and sometimes terribly unfair? I put the hook and belt in an envelope. I took something else from the room and put it in a bag. It was against all my training, but I couldn't help it. I counted the number of empty beer cans in the living room, kitchen, bathroom, and driveway. I sorted through the kitchen trash, making sure my count was correct.

The hospital awaited. Detectives wanted photographs of her ligature marks, to make sure they matched the belt I collected. She was in a neck brace, on a ventilator, unconscious. Fireworks' explosions replaced by mechanical beeps. Her fingernails painted a bright fiery red, her hair spilling over the sheet. She had carrot-colored hair. Anne of Green Gables hair. I'll call her Anne. I whispered, "Hey, Anne. We're going to take this neck brace off of you. It's okay, sweetie. My name is Laura. I'm just going to take some pictures of you. You're going to be just fine. I'm with the police department. Have you ever seen CSI?" I was babbling to a girl in a coma. She didn't answer me. The nurses removed the neck brace and tilted her head back so I could get the best possible shot of the red lines on her neck. A gurgling sound came from her chest. I snapped three quick pictures. That was all. My job was done. I would write it all up, and if a court case against her father for negligence occurred, my photographs and beer can count would be admitted.

The nurses were waiting for me to leave. I held up the bag I had taken from her room. They nodded. I sat down by her bed.

"Hey Anne. I brought you something." I smoothed her hair off her face as I spoke. "I know you can't open your eyes right now, but maybe you'd like to feel this next to you." There had been a stuffed panda bear on her bed. The only toy on it, which made it stand out. The other beds were all covered with cars and dolls and clothes. I put the panda next to her right hand at her side and curled her fingers around a paw and made a wish.

How old do you have to be before struggling against the current seems futile? I made a wish that Anne would live to see her ninth birthday in three months.

CHAPTER TWENTY-NINE

Hotel Etiquette

It started out so simply. A man breaks out of a window of a hotel, unlocks it, and crawls through. He then liberates the TV from the living area (it's a hotel suite) and the one from the cabinet in the bedroom. He takes those TVs and puts them in his car. He moves on to the next suite and does the same thing. Unfortunately for him, someone sees him and calls 911. The police arrive just as he is loading the fourth TV into his car. The police come around and ask him to put the TV down and to place his hands behind his back. They are still talking to him when I arrive on scene. They ask him what he is doing with these stolen TVs, to which he replies, "I didn't know they were stolen."

Now, I looked at the broken windows, the four TVs in his car, the mangled wooden board that one of the TVs was still bolted to, and I decided I did not believe his story. I think he did know these TVs were stolen. In fact, I think his intention was to steal the TVs. Because while hotels will generally overlook it if you take the shower cap, I believe there is a line somewhere between accessories and furniture, and TVs definitely fall under the latter category. I think they also might object to you taking the shower cap if you break the windows to get to it, or if you are not currently staying in said hotel as a guest. These are the rules of hotel etiquette that everyone should know. You can take the free packet of coffee, you cannot take the coffee maker. You can take the shampoo on the end table, you cannot take the end table itself. You can take the light bulb out of the lamp, but you must leave the lamp behind. This isn't rocket science. If you can possibly use up an object while you're in the hotel, you can keep it. If you can't use it up (like the bed, the bed is never used up), then it stays in the hotel, perhaps for the future use of another guest, since hotels generally like it if a room is used by more than one person in its existence.

So I photographed the mess in the two suites that my poor

inexperienced thief had broken into. I noticed the bolt cutters in his car that he had used to liberate the TVs from their TV stands. I photographed those too. Here's another hint. If you have to use bolt cutters to remove an object from the hotel room, that object is supposed to remain with the room. Just like if you have to use a hammer to break the window to enter the room, you probably aren't supposed to be entering that room. This man had somehow missed that lesson in school. I'm guessing he was in the bathroom smoking some sort of substance during that class period. Just a feeling I had from him. As I returned the unstolen TVs to the hotel owner and called it a day, the suspect turned to me and said with panic in his voice, "No one told me they were stolen!"

I paused. I turned. I spoke. "No sir. No one told you they were stolen because you were the one stealing them."

He nodded and I noticed his eyes had a glassy sheen to them.

"Well, that's okay then. Even if I tell myself something, I never listen." I nodded back at him. I'm not sure if that's the best thing I could have said to him; after all, I could have told him to stop taking things that didn't belong to him, or that required bolt cutters to remove, but it was the best my befuddled brain could muster, under the circumstances. As I left, he was asking if he could keep the remote controls in his pockets since they were universal remotes and might work the prison TV....

CHAPTER THIRTY
Sing-Sing

I sing on my way to crime scenes. The police radio and NPR tend to conflict with each other, and riding in silence on my way to someone else's tragedy isn't an option I care to entertain, thus, I sing. Sometimes I catch people staring at me as we're stopped at a light. At these times, I pretend I'm talking into my police radio, and then nod to the citizen in the car watching me. But for the most part, I ignore the outside world. I get my call—rape, robbery, cutting, domestic violence—climb into my van, and sing. I sing the same song every time. I never intended to start my own personal tradition. I always tried to sing some variety—Broadway show tunes, often. "Macavity" from Cats is a good one (about a master criminal); "Look Down" and "Master of the House" from Les Misérables are also about criminals. Ellis Paul's song "I'm the One to Save" mentions Alcatraz. But whenever I shut my internal jukebox off, the same song comes out. I sing it as soon as the engine starts, before I even realize notes are emerging from my mouth. It's a simple song really. My earliest memory of it comes from a M*A*S*H episode. The camp is celebrating Christmas and Hawkeye is honoring Father Mulcahy. I see them in my mind: Hawkeye singing, nose red, eyes moist, no laughter in his face, and Father Mulcahy rubbing his eyeglasses on his shirt in his own modest way. I sang this song in seventh grade chorus and for once, we were in tune and held the harmonies together. It's one of the few phrases I know in Latin. Dona nobis pacem. Give us peace. I sing this, I plead this, before every scene of personal tragedy. Give us peace.

Today is September 11th. It's the anniversary of several men with boxcutters killing more than three thousand people in this country. More than three thousand more of our citizens have died attempting to root out the people who allowed the initial attack to occur. Ten thousand citizens of Iraq who had no part in the deaths of those original three thousand have died. The women of Afghanistan are still afraid to walk outside without a burqa. The citizens of Iraq are used to the bombs now. A genocide is occurring in the Sudan. More than a million people are dying in refugee camps. Thousands are being held by our own government in Cuba. North Korea tested a nuclear bomb. Dona nobis pacem.

The Olympics just ended. Each winner heard his or her national anthem. Perhaps it's time we stopped listening to national anthems and started working on a global one. To realize that for better or for worse, we're all on this planet together. And we can make it a better place for everyone, or we can bomb it into nuclear waste. I have the perfect song for our global anthem. I sing it every day. It's in a language no one uses anymore, so no one can claim it. And it speaks to the heart of all those people who have seen one too many bombs, one too many reports on casualties and collateral damage—or one too many crime scenes.

They filed back into the room in a somber line. They did not look at anyone. The note was passed to the judge, who opened it, and handed it back to the bailiff.

"On the sole count of the indictment, aggravated rape, how do you find?"

"We find the defendant not guilty."

His shoulders started to shake and tears fell from his eyes. His mother embraced him. His buddies clapped him on the back. I sat in the back of the courtroom and could not breathe. Just breathe, I told myself. Just breathe. But I couldn't make myself do it. I felt a hand on my shoulder and looked up to see Pat there.

"We can't judge the job we do by a jury. Juries make lousy decisions sometimes. You just have to remember. We'll get him. He'll mess up one time, and we'll get him eventually."

Every cop says that when a suspect eludes capture, and every prosecutor says it when they lose a case in court. I watched the victim slink out of the courtroom by the side door. Her name was Jennifer. It's a logic puzzle, I told myself. How many Jennifers equal eventually?

CHAPTER THIRTY-ONE
All Washed Up

The problem: WPD lab employees are underpaid and lack training opportunities and thus their morale is low. The solution: We needed to wash our police vehicles more often. At least according to a memo we received from our fearless leader.

Apparently, we had low morale because our crime scene vans looked dirty and thus gave the public a bad impression. I had no idea this was the reason why we complained bitterly about the lack of promotion opportunities and training, and the low pay. How silly of me to have suggested that we ask for a larger budget to buy needed equipment such as fingerprint brushes and better UV lights. We had been told we didn't have the money for these items. Fair enough. Budgets were tight all over the state. However, we apparently had hundreds of dollars to spend on car washes. The memo said each investigator must wash his or her vehicle twice a month. There were four vans, and each van was assigned to one investigator per shift. There were three shifts. Let's all do the math together. That meant that each van would be washed six times a month. (My personal car gets washed about two times a year.) At a cost of $5 a wash, that was $120 a month on car washes. For a whole year, that would be $1,440. That amount would have bought us more than fifty fingerprint brushes or three UV lights, or better yet, we could have sent two people to the latest IAI conference in St. Louis.

See now, I knew these vans got dirty, but did they really need to be washed six times a month? That was more than once a week! And I knew that I generally needed a shower after I got off of work each day, but that was because I had to actually physically enter the crime scenes. I got the blood and filth of the scenes on my clothes, I sweated, and I crawled through basements with cobwebs. The van stayed parked outside. The van just got to sit there on the pavement. Quite frankly, I didn't think the van was pulling its full weight at these scenes. And it certainly didn't need to be washed every five days.

The real irony here was that we could wash our vans for free. And I frequently did. The central maintenance facility had a wash bay with soap, a high-powered water hose, and rags that we could use to wash our vans. But since we didn't get receipts from washing the vans there, we weren't allowed to use that anymore.

So one day I was told that I was falling behind on the job by washing the van myself and that I should take it to a brushless wash facility. Fine by me. I drove the van to the car wash we were supposed to use (all the way down south of town—using about a gallon of city-paid gas to get there). I told the girl at the counter that I needed a police vehicle wash, and she keyed up the amount and swiped the card through the card reader (charging the city $5). I drove the van around to the wash site, punched in the key code, and drove into the wash. The water spray began, the soap spray came on ... and then it all stopped. And one arm of the water spray machine came crashing down on the hood of the van. Luckily, it was foam covered, so when I say "came crashing down," I really mean that it bounced lightly upon the hood, causing no damage whatsoever. And there I sat in my sudsy van, wondering what on earth had happened.

Have you ever contemplated getting out of your car in the middle of a stopped car wash? What if it blasts to life again? Then I'd be a sudsy wet crime scene investigator, which might be great for a porn video, but certainly seemed a tad inappropriate for my current job. So there I sat. Trapped in the car wash. Listening to the police radio, hoping I would not get called to a scene. I felt like calling the lab director and explaining the situation to him. After all, I needed some guidance on my next move, and we certainly hadn't covered this in any training I had ever taken. But instead I drove forward, letting the foam arm of the water spray machine bounce foamily, happily, up and over my van. I felt like I was driving the van version of the Stay-Puft Marshmallow Man. The girl at the front counter told me that she had a water hose I could use to rinse the foam off, but that the van would look pretty bad because they used a special soap that needed a solvent to stop it from streaking. She could call up another location and tell them I would be coming over soon.

"No, no," I stated. Just let me rinse off the van. Let it be streaked.

The van now looked vaguely reminiscent of a fat blue zebra. But after all, I had done my part. I had cost the city $5, and had my receipt to prove it. I drove back to the lab, past the central maintenance facility, where I had previously washed my van to a sparkling shine, and parked it next to the lab director's car in the parking lot, handed him the receipt, and set about typing my reports.

My morale for the rest of the day was quite upbeat.

CHAPTER THIRTY-TWO

Forecasting the Future

It's possible that I'm getting burned out, I thought as I looked at the pieces of the broken footwear cast on the ground in front of me. The broken cast of a footwear impression that wasn't broken when I had picked it up from the ground, but was most definitely broken now. I had spent the last hour and a half waiting for this now-broken cast to dry so that I could pry it out of the dirt, so that I could collect it and submit it to the detective investigating the case, so that he could not send it off for comparison because we didn't have an examiner for footwear impressions. It wasn't that I was burned out, I decided. It's that I was disillusioned. I hadn't walked into this job with expectations generated by television shows, because the shows hadn't existed when I started my graduate program, so I knew the reality before the drama came out. It was that I knew what could be done, and what was done, and those were two entirely different things.

I had recently had a burglary case that had been closed before the detective received my report saying I had usable fingerprints from the scene. I had cases where footwear comparisons were possible, but as our firearms examiner was also the footwear and tool marks examiner, the chances of him getting around to looking at the footwear from these cases were slim at best, as he was already overworked from the sheer number of shootings in the city. (Most of the shootings were just drive-bys that didn't hit anyone, because the gang members all liked to hold their guns sideways when they shot so that they looked cool.)

I had spent two full hours on that footwear cast. The person who had robbed the restaurant had worn gloves and hadn't provided any clue as to his identity. In addition, the restaurant didn't have security cameras. But our patrol officers and detectives were never deterred by those sorts of setbacks and had already gotten word from several informants that they might want to look at a certain individual in conjunction with the crime. And while having a suspect is nice, having something to tie him to the crime is nicer.

The maître d' of the restaurant had run out after the suspect and watched him dash across the grass, slip on the mud, right himself, and continue the flight. And patrol noticed some marks in the mud, including a skid mark from a shoe, and a perfect shoe impression a few feet beyond.

I couldn't do anything much with the skid mark except to photograph it and measure it, but the shoe impression was another matter. For two hours I worked on that impression. After first setting up the tripod and inverting the center piece that holds the camera, I spent painstaking minutes with a flashlight and synchronized flash unit to properly light the impression for maximum clarity and detail, in case something should go wrong with the casting of the impression. I measured it. I sketched it. And then I made a cast of it.

We used dental stone in the crime lab for casting impressions. It was called dental stone because it was the same substance dentists used for making impressions of people's mouths for dentures and such. Some people put the powder and the water in a plastic Ziploc bag, mixed it up by squeezing the bag, and then poured it out over the impression. I had once attempted to do this, which was when we all learned that Laura's hands are freakishly small and quite weak and she's not able to mix things by hand. It had come out all lumpy and that doesn't work well when you need to pour the mixture smoothly over the impression so as not to mess it up.

Luckily, Patti took pity on me and pointed out that she didn't mix it this way either. She used rubber bowls and a tongue depressor to mix and pour. And then, to clean the bowls all you had to do was wait for the mixture to harden, and turn the bowl inside out. The excess hardened dental stone popped right out.

So I had mixed and poured and everything had gone according to plan, except that it didn't want to harden. Apparently the 99% humidity was enough to make the dental stone decide that it quite liked to be in liquid form and really, there was no need to harden. It would just remain there, like a little puddle of beige fungus. I borrowed a handheld battery-operated fan from the officer at the scene, who had one due to the heat and humidity of Wichita summers, and tried to cool off and thus harden the cast.

After ninty minutes of fanning, cursing, and ignoring the cast in favor of chatting with local passers-by who wanted to know if they could ride along in the crime scene van, and if it really was just like how CSI showed it on TV, the cast hardened enough to pry it from the ground. This involves digging in the soil a few inches away from the cast and then pushing diagonally upward toward the cast with a trowel or digging fork. If done improperly, it can break the still fragile cast, so it must be done with painstaking care.

Sweat trickled down my back as I dug, and once again, the lack of air-conditioned uniforms seemed to me to be an oversight of monumental proportions by the garment industry at large.

Finally, triumphant, I held the cast in my hand. It had come out perfectly, and now just needed to be placed in a box for evidentiary purposes. I strode purposefully to the van, and as I reached it, I dropped the cast. I just … dropped it. No idea how my hand lost its grip or why, just a slow-motion feeling as it left my fingers and dropped to the ground, where it broke in two.

Okay, I told myself. Breathe. It's okay. It only broke in two pieces … and no one saw that.

This was important. It's important that no one see when I do something so boneheaded that I could be mocked by everyone in the department for years to come. Like the time I was driving to a scene in the middle of an ice storm and attempted to turn left, only to have the van do a lazy circle on the ice in the middle of the intersection because it had lost all traction. As I spun about, I noticed that there was no one else on the road (because of the aforementioned ice storm) and as such, since I couldn't do anything about the spin, I should just sit back and enjoy it.

By sheer luck the van had ended up facing in the direction in which I wanted to travel, so after a brief moment of, "Hey! No one saw that," I drove off to the scene whistling a jaunty tune.

After scooping up the pieces of the cast and putting them in a box, I drove off. It really doesn't matter, I told myself. No one is going to bother looking at it anyway. But there was so much more that could have been done with it if the detectives had just given it a chance. In Arlington, Virginia, I knew a detective who had once taken a nice footwear impression and scanned it into the computer. He had then typed the suspect's name, social security number, date of birth, and address onto the scanned image and brought it into the interrogation room, where he slammed it down on the desk and told the suspect that Walmart, using their shoe purchase database, had just confirmed that it was the suspect's shoeprint at the scene. The suspect confessed on the spot. That was the sort of originality I wanted to be part of.

When I had first come to Wichita, they had promised me that I could intern with the firearms and tool marks examiner, because that was where my interest really lay. But after a year and change of promises but no action, the time had come for me to look around for better options. I had interviewed out in Portland and had sent a resume off to a private forensics lab in London. It was time for me to leave. It was time for a change. The only thing that gave me pause was that leaving Wichita would mean leaving James. And that thought broke my heart. As long as he shared joint custody with his ex-wife of their son, he would never be able to follow me if I moved, and I would never ask him to. I had seen too many children with absentee fathers in this job. I didn't need to create one more.

When I got back to the lab, I noticed that in spite of the cast being in two pieces, it really was an excellent cast. The detail was crystal clear and several marks on the cast were easily identifiable as unique to the particular sneaker. I made note of it in my report and provided photographs of both the original impression in the mud and the cast I had made. I was informed the next day that the suspect had confessed, and that he'd probably have a plea deal lined up within the week. No one had even looked at the cast. And that was the way it went for most scenes. The evidence that we collected wasn't used or tested, and it really didn't matter anyway. It was enough to drive a girl straight to Portland, or London, or any other place where I would feel more appreciated. I just needed teleportation to be invented first so I could come home to dinner with James each night.

CHAPTER THIRTY-THREE

Click Your Heels Three Times

The telephone rang at 7:15 in the morning, which was just plain wrong. No one should ever call a second-shift CSI at 7:15 in the morning, because that's right when the best sleep is to be had. The sleep that says, "Hey, I know that most of the rest of the world is awake, but I get to sleep in, so ha-ha to all you high school gym teachers who made me get up at the crack of dawn to go play volleyball, even though that wasn't really much of a way to stay physically fit, because now I have a job where I can sleep in."

Not that I was happy with the job. Things had been coming to a head for a while, and I had even recently applied to be an adjunct teacher over at one of the community colleges. The politics of the police department, combined with my mounting frustration over the uselessness that I felt at most crime scenes, had taken away much of my initial joy and enthusiasm. Were it not for the Vagabond regulars and my Unitarian friends and James, I would have been miserable. As it was, I spent eight hours of my days being miserable at work, followed by six or seven hours of joy with James or my friends. James and I had discussed the implications of quitting my job in favor of working at the college. I would lose all my health insurance benefits and my pension plan. I would be making far less money. He mentioned that perhaps when my lease was up, I might move in with him. And although the thought frightened me, I was elated at the same time. For the first time in my life, I envisioned growing old with someone. But I had to get out of my job. It was slowly destroying my faith in people, though my mother and friends were always quick to remind me that I saw the worst side of people, and I had to remember that my coworkers and I were on the side of justice, that we were the ones representing the good side of people.

I looked at the telephone number on the display screen. Area code 202? I knew that area code. My sleep-fogged brain attempted to make some sort of logical connection but came up with none. I had missed the call, but hit the callback button because anyone calling long distance at 7:15 in the morning must need something urgently.

"Hi, this is Laura Merz, and I just missed a call from this number…"

"Laura!" exclaimed the voice on the other end of the line. "Laura, this is Cheryl Marsh. From the Naval Criminal Investigative Service. We have a position to offer you!"

The excitement in her voice cut through my confusion. Cheryl? NCIS? Was I dreaming? I had given up on them only the day before. My mom and I had talked, and I'd told her that NCIS was most likely no longer an option. It had been two years since my application had first entered their system and it had just been too long. I dropped the phone and dived for it, scaring Pyewacket in the process. He had been on the bed beside me and my dive over him was enough for him to disappear into the closet where only two luminous large eyes could be seen for the next several hours. I would apologize to him later, but right now, more important things were at hand.

"We want you to come to Camp Pendleton on the 18th. I know it wasn't one of your top choices when you applied, but it's a good training office…" her voice trailed off. Yes! Yes! Oh my goodness, yes! I don't know if other new federal agents jump up and down and squeal excitedly upon hearing the news that they were being hired, but I did. I had no idea where Camp Pendleton was. I had never even heard of it, but right then it was Mecca. It was Eden. It was Not-the-Wichita-Police-Department. I managed to get a few of the details together and provided Cheryl with a fax number where she could send the documents I would need to sign.

I attempted to sound grateful and dignified while jumping. And then I called my mom. Because every new federal agent should call her mom at times like these. My mother, who had laughed and cried with me during my time in Kansas, who had lived through most of my trials and tribulations via telephone, had not a clue what I was saying. My voice had reached pitches that only dogs could hear. Breathe, I told myself. Just breathe. And as we rejoiced and I hung up the phone, the squeals of joy turned sadder into sobbing. Because I was leaving Wichita. And I loved Wichita. I loved my Vagabond friends, my Unitarians, Dave, Heather—and James. Especially James. Mainly James. I had built a family here. I called James and asked him to meet me for lunch. The 18th was only three weeks away. I needed to quit my job, plan to move the rest of the way across the country, and get out there in twenty-one days. I had three weeks to say goodbye to him.

If he asks me, I told myself, I'll stay. If he asks me, I will grow old with him, and I will help him raise his children. If he asks me to, I will. I knew that to be true, and I knew it to be one path that I wanted. It was just… not the only path that I wanted. An unstoppable force had met an immovable object. I had to leave, and James could not. As we sat at the table, I took his hand and told him about the telephone call. He gave the perfect answer. He hugged me and said, "Congratulations!" But his smile, wide enough to reach to California, never made it to his eyes. He volunteered to take care of Pyewacket while I was in training in Georgia for four months to learn to be an agent.

He didn't ask me to stay. I wondered if he even considered asking me to. Was he letting me go to see if I returned? How was it possible to be so excited and so miserable at the same time? I didn't know if he wanted a long-distance relationship, but I suspected that though we might promise to try to hold onto what we had, it was nearly impossible to hold onto someone fifteen hundred miles away, especially if the chance of being reunited during the ensuing twenty years was slim. There aren't many Navy bases in Kansas. (It has something to do with the large boats needing water to sail upon.) So getting stationed there, with him, wasn't a possibility I could reasonably consider. I was leaving Wichita. I was leaving James. I would probably never find out who the hell belonged to that right tibia, or if the city and police would settle their differences over wages.

When James hugged me at the end of our lunch, it lasted longer than normal. I felt his shoulders shake and I clutched him to me after he moved to let go. The time had come to take my car the rest of the way across the country. Wichita had seen me halfway there. I would have to make the other half of the trip alone.

Epilogue

Art looked at me expectantly. "You know how to use one of these?" he asked.

It was my first week at Camp Pendleton in sunny southern California after graduation from the Federal Law Enforcement Training Center. I had spent the past four months learning to drive cars at high speeds I had never attempted in my everyday life, shoot handguns and shotguns, perform self-defense moves, and interrogate suspects.

I was now assigned to Art for the next six weeks, as he was my field training agent. He would let people know if I had what it took in the field to be a good agent. He had about twenty years with the agency, and a twinkle in his eye that reminded me of Pat. When the call came in that a rape had occurred on the base, he figured this would be a good chance to observe me in action, and the major case response team rolled out to the house.

Art handed me the alternate light source, and we strode up to the residence. I smiled at him and nodded. Yes, I knew how to use it. The heft of it felt right in my hand.

The Marine MP at the house appeared to be new and very unsure of himself as he secured the residence. He fidgeted with his uniform and kept fingering the gun on his hip. I guessed this was his first scene. He couldn't have been more than twenty-one or twenty-two, which seemed very young to me in my whopping twenty-six years of life. I touched his shoulder.

"Breathe," I told him. "Just breathe."

About the Author

Laura Merz became a Special Agent with the Naval Criminal Investigative Service (NCIS) after leaving her job as a Crime Scene Investigator (CSI) with the Wichita Police Department. She jokes she did not really switch jobs, she just changed TV shows. When people ask her how she ended up as a CSI or NCIS Special Agent she'll tell them a completely true set of incredibly ridiculous circumstances involving a guy who broke his leg in the 1930s, sparrows, and Columbia University not honoring AP math credits from high schools, that lead to her current career. (Don't worry, that'll all be in the next book). She is a member of the Association of Threat Assessment Professionals and is passionate about imparting information in story form, rather than PowerPoint bullets. She has moved to Kansas, California, Japan, and now Italy in pursuit of stories to tell and crimes to investigate.

www.ingramcontent.com/pod-product-compliance
Lightning Source LLC
Chambersburg PA
CBHW060422260626
47161CB00005B/1736